Praise for Marie M
Murder Mysteries

GAME DRIVE

"Moore's safari mystery proves that humans are more dangerous than wild animals! Compelling and well-written."
—Sarah Wisseman, author of the Lisa Donahue Archaeological Mysteries

"With a vividly picturesque landscape as the backdrop and surrounded by a great supporting cast, this safari mystery adventure is an amazing ride and I'm looking forward to their next expedition in this terrific series."
—Dru's Book Musings

SHORE EXCURSION

"An appealing heroine tangles with murder and romantic interludes gone wrong in a tartly funny take-off on tour travel, with more twists than a conga line. Readers will be enthralled."
—Carolyn Hart, author of the *Death on Demand* series

"Anyone who has been on a cruise ship will appreciate the behind-the-scenes look at what goes on in *Shore Excursion*, murders notwithstanding. Sidney Marsh is an engaging amateur sleuth and the mystery in which she finds herself is creatively devised and vividly drawn. (The international setting helps as does a diverse cast of suspects.) Readers will certainly welcome back Sidney on another tour."
—Mysterious Reviews, June, 2012

"I love a good mystery and this debut mystery of Marie Moore's is just that ... A really good book and I give it a 5, so Marie you have a bestseller on your hand as I see it."
—Edna Tollison's Reviews

"Beware all mystery writers. Marie Moore has now joined your genre with her well-told tale, *Shore Excursion* ...

This cleverly written mystery with its elaborate attention to detail will catch your imagination within a few pages .... It is hard to believe that *Shore Excursion* is Marie Moore's first mystery."

—Regis Schilken , Blogcritics

"A wonderful amateur sleuth mystery starring an intrepid heroine and a quirky support cast. Armchair travelers will enjoy cruising the fjords of Scandinavia. Sidney makes too many mistakes on her first inquiry, but like the Mississippi bulldog she is, she keeps on trying; her error-filled efforts bring plausibility to a magical mystery tour of Scandinavia."

—Harriet Klausner

"I really enjoyed this book.... The author gives a lot of handy tips for international travel. That aspect of the book was just as interesting as the mystery .... A lot of times, I have a fairly good idea of the motive behind the murder. But this one, not a clue."

—The Bluestocking Guide

"*Shore Excursion* took me on a cruise filled with danger, secrets, excitement and intrigue. I can't wait to go on another trip with Sidney."

—Carol's Bookshelf

"*Shore Excursion* combines both my desire for a cruise with my love of a mystery .... I have to say, for a first time book, this was really good."

—Lenore Webb, theysayimnuts.blogspot.com

"Moore leads us on a merry chase happily trying to figure out whodunnit, yet wanting to jump ship. Graced with humor, a striking cast of characters, masterful deception and really good writing, I can't wait for the next in this appealing new series!"

—Wendy Hines, Minding Spot

"Sidney will keep you on your toes and guessing as she goes about sleuthing; this is a highly entertaining and fast-paced read. This first book of Marie Moore is sure to be a great seller and leaves you highly anticipating the next mystery!"

—Lauri Meinhardt, Knits and Reads

"This delightful little mystery will amuse most lovers of the cozy mystery genre and of Agatha Christie's stories .... I can easily recommend this to mystery lovers. It'd make a great beach read."

—Valentina Cano, Carrabosse's Library

"This is an exciting suspense/thriller with all the ingredients to keep readers at the edge of their seats. It has romance, adventure and quite a bit of mystery all tossed into one huge, compelling story."

—Yvonne, *Socrates Book Reviews*

"If you enjoy travel, especially to different countries, you will enjoy this book. It is light and funny, filled with enjoyable experiences. There is a bit of suspense and danger as well, but it does not overshadow the sense of fun imbued with the telling."

—Leslie Ann Wright, *BlogCritics* and *Tictoc*

"If you love mysteries and want to take a ride on a cruise ship (not literally of course) to solve a murder mystery or two, then you definitely need to read this book."

—Franjessca Papillion, Book Lovin' Mamas

"*Shore Excursion* is what would have happened if Nancy Drew had decided to become a travel agent. Sidney Marsh is stubborn and sassy."

—Chaundra Haun, Unabridged Bookshelf

"Moore's debut novel is a winner. Her world was so descriptive that I felt as though I was on the journey with the

High Steppers. Also, the conclusion was satisfying; especially with the unexpected twist just when I thought the mystery was solved."

—Kellie, Simply Stacie

"A crime novel that focuses on people and relationships rather than violence and gore. There's suspense, humour, romance and action. It entertained me and made me laugh while I also pondered 'who dunnit'"

—Dianne Ascroft, Author, Toronto, Canada.

"Brava Ms. Moore!.... A trip you wouldn't want to miss with a cast and crew you won't soon forget. The twists and turns, triumphs and stumbles, all add up to a grand reading adventure."

—Satisfaction for Insatiable Readers

"With a well-developed plot, a determined heroine, a great supporting cast and the perfect setting for murder, this was a good read .... I like the characters and the tone of the story and I hope there are more adventures with Sidney in this enjoyable debut series."

—Dru Ann Love, *Dru's Cozy Report, CozyChicksBlog*

Game Drive

Game Drive

MARIE MOORE

Seattle, WA

CAMEL
PRESS

Camel Press
PO Box 70515
Seattle, WA 98127

For more information go to: www.camelpress.com
www.mariemooremysteries.com

Cover design by Sabrina Sun

Game Drive
Copyright © 2013 by Marie Moore

ISBN: 978-1-60381-961-9 (Trade Paper)
ISBN: 978-1-60381-962-6 (eBook)

Library of Congress Control Number: 2013932448

Printed in the United States of America

Acknowledgments

My sincere thanks for their help on *Game Drive* go to my faithful and tireless agents and friends, Victoria Marini and Jane Gelfman, and to the editorial team at Camel Press; Catherine Treadgold, Publisher and Editor, Acquiring Editor Jennifer McCord and their assistant, Emily, for their time and efforts in the publication of this book.

I also want to thank all of the wonderful friends, Linda Seale, Lockie York, Kathy Elgin, the ladies of the Holly Springs Garden Club, Grace and James McLaren, Marie and Ryan Holder, Susanna and Tudor Moldoveanu, Walter Cooper and Lois Sandusky, Beverly Massey, Charlene Roberts, Joan and Leslie Sigman, and Ruff and Susan Fant, who gave such fantastic parties and events in celebration of the release of my first novel, *Shore Excursion*.

I am also extremely grateful to Linn Sitler, Lyla McAlexander, Jonathan, Angie, Tom and Cindy Pittman, Terri Smith, and Amanda Tatro of Click Magazine, Charlotte Bray and Macon Wilson of The Booksellers at Laurelwood, Emily Gatlin and Jack Reed of Reed's Gum Tree Books, Judy Spencer, Helen Hancock, Joe Hickman of Lemuria Books, Ward Emling, Linda Jones and Barbara Taylor of *The South Reporter*, Lois Sandusky, William Mauldin, Philip Rucker, John Beifuss, Stephen Usery, Bruce McMillin, Marybeth Conley, Wang-Ying Glasgow, Jan Oglesby, Frank Hurdle, Donna Dafur-Lindsey, Sharlinda Murphy, Virginia Goza, Dottie Kerstine, and Susan Reichert of *Southern Writer's*

Magazine for their loyal support and help in the promotion of my books.

Special thanks go also to all the great reviewers, bloggers and fellow writers who gave a fledgling author a much-needed boost, particularly 2013 Amelia Award winner Carolyn Hart and archeological mystery author Sarah Wisseman. I would also like to tell all those who nominated *Shore Excursion* for an Agatha Award as Best First Novel how very much I appreciate such a compliment to my work.

And as always, my deepest gratitude is reserved for my precious girls, Marie and Susanna, and for Kathryn, who opened the door and made it all possible.

But most of all, I am eternally grateful for my husband, Rook, who has cheered me on every step of the way.

For Alex, my little animal expert,
and in memory of all the cats in my life,
Jean, Tanny, Rick, Lucky, Bessie, Sammie, Mikey,
Big Stripes, and The Red Cat.

Then Kolokolo Bird said, with a mournful cry,
"Go to the banks of the great grey-green, greasy Limpopo
River, all set about with fever-trees and find out."

—Rudyard Kipling, *Just So Stories*, "The Elephant's Child"

"Who named this place 'Leopard Dance'?"

"I did, darling, I did. In the very beginning, I named it. I am fascinated with leopards. Though terribly dangerous, they are also beautiful. And the beast is a self-sufficient, solitary creature. Like you. And like me. *Ingwe*, they call the cat. That is a Zulu word. It means both king and leopard. One must be careful in the presence of *Ingwe*."

Once again, Winsome's words came to mind.

"Then there may be truth in what your drivers say."

"And what is that, my love? What do my drivers say?"

"They say, 'He who dines with the leopard is liable to be eaten.' "

He laughed then, and smiled down at me, pulling me closer.

"That's an old native saying, my dear, and it may be true. One must be very careful with a leopard."

1

A goose ran right smack over my grave on Monday morning, just as I climbed out of the subway at Prince Street in Lower Manhattan. I shuddered all over, shook it off, and headed uptown to my office.

That's what we call it, anyway, back home in Dixie, when shivers just shoot down your spine for no good reason. There's probably some real name for it, some medical term. I just don't know it.

But you know what I mean, don't you?

Some might say it was the brisk north wind that set me shivering, but they would be wrong. The wind was icy, no doubt about that. It sent my long, black hair swirling all around and blew my skinny little coat open. But the wind wasn't the problem. No, not the wind.

I don't have second sight, and I didn't have a big premonition or anything, but I should have.

And every time I get that old, cold, nasty feeling, something bad happens pretty soon, trust me.

♓

When I arrived ten minutes late for work at the travel agency, the faded posters in the windows had been replaced with a giant zebra-striped banner that read, "Need a getaway? *Hakuna matata!* Give us a call!"

I pushed open the glass door and heard African chants and drumbeats instead of the usual elevator music. The walls were plastered with tribal masks and lion posters. The standard shots of the Eiffel Tower and Big Ben were gone.

My name is Sidney Marsh, and I'm a travel agent. I came to New York eight years ago for a summer internship with an agency and fell in love with the City, so I worked overtime until I managed to turn that little job into a career.

My mother, back home in Mississippi, nearly passed out over the idea of blowing off college and sorority rush for Manhattan, but she's finally gotten used to it. Sort of.

Which is good, because I love New York and I'm not going back home anytime soon.

The agency I work for is called Itchy Feet Travel. Our name sounds kind of goofy, but it appeals to people and we're pretty successful, even in tough times. We work really hard to send folks around the world happily and safely, usually with success. I have to admit that my last trip out, a Scandinavian cruise, was a big bomb. I refuse to think about that. What happened on that ship was totally not my fault, no matter what my boss thinks.

I was used to a pretty blah-looking office, so the Tarzan motif came as a complete surprise. Because most of our business is done over the phone or on computers, we don't do a lot of decorating for walk-ins. The African transformation was a stunner.

Roz, our receptionist, had a Tilley hat—a packable tan safari hat with a chin strap—crammed down on her orange do and a tan safari vest stretched across her double-Ds.

She did not look happy.

"Hi, hon, bedda hurry. You're late for the staff meeting. Everybody else is in there awready. Big Bwana himself is on his way over. Be here in five, his driver said. Bedda move it!"

Wait a minute.

"There's a staff meeting? What staff meeting? Nobody told me about any staff meeting."

"One of these days, hon, ya gotta start checkin' the sign-in announcements on ya computah. It's been on there for two, three weeks. This is the big surprise Diana's been hintin' around about. The new product launch. Like I said, His Majesty himself is comin' over to explain it."

She pulled a mirror from her desk drawer and started clumping on more mascara.

"Wish I had those big eyes of yours, Sidney. Then I wouldn't have to mess with this crap. It never stays on like it should, no matter what kind I buy. By the end of the day I look just like a raccoon. Bedda hurry on in, hon. Everyone else is there awready. What I'm tryin' to say is, if you're not in your chair when His Highness gets here, your ass is grass."

I threw my stuff down on my desk, smoothed my wild black hair, swirled on some lipstick, and scooted down the hall to the conference room. See, even though I've been living in New York for a while now, deep down, I'm still a Southern girl. Roz is right. I have long enough lashes that I don't have to wear much eye makeup, but Dixie darlings *always* take time for lipstick.

I eased the door open, hoping to slip inside unnoticed. No luck. All eyes were on me.

"Well, Sidney. How very nice of you to join us this morning. Did you oversleep, dear, are you ill, or was your train just late again?"

Diana. Our manager. My boss. She stared at me, her cold blue eyes now icy slits, tapping her pen on the table. Diana, dressed in a flowing orange caftan, her silver hair pulled back into a smooth knot and secured with some kind of bone or tooth or something. Diana. Bitch Queen of the Universe, according to my best friend and colleague, Jay Wilson.

Jay had arrived ahead of me for a change, and was already in his seat in the back corner of the room. Giving me a wide smile, he pointed to his watch. He overwhelmed the folding chair, his big frame dwarfing the metal, his shock of red hair flaming against the taupe walls.

Before I could respond, Mr. Silverstein, owner of our

agency, burst through the door with his wormy little assistant Andre fluttering along in his wake. Diana jumped up from the table to greet them and, in all her gooey gushing, forgot about me.

Silverstein and his shadow must have swung by the wardrobe department at Central Casting on their way over. They were both decked out in full safari gear. I fervently hoped that they weren't going to insist on pith hats and khaki shorts for all of us. I admired my new black heels, Chanel knockoffs, purchased over the weekend in Lower Manhattan. I had no plans to trade those in for safari boots.

"Jambo, ladies and gentlemen, JAMBOOOOOOOOO!" Silverstein boomed. Everyone jumped.

Silverstein is a big boy, tall, with wide shoulders. He has the plummy bass voice of an anchorman, abundant curly silver hair, and the deep tan of an outdoorsman. The tan is fake, though. I know from a reliable source that it is sprayed on regularly at a salon near his office on Sixth Avenue.

Our leader has sharp brown eyes behind thick silver wire-rims and a pretty good build for his age. From the way he was posing, he clearly thought his bum and legs looked great in the British tan shorts and tall socks he was wearing.

It was rare to see Diana so flustered, but she was in the presence of the Mighty One. When he barked at her to dim the lights for his PowerPoint presentation, she tripped over her caftan and barely regained her balance before crashing into the wall. Jay winked at me and snorted a laugh.

"Your attention, please, ladies and gentlemen," Silverstein began, nodding to Andre, who brought up the first photo on the screen—a postcard shot of elephants at sunrise.

"Welcome to 'Fantastic Africa,' a luxurious adventure tour custom designed just for our IFT clients, with, of course, as always, that special Silverstein touch and attention to detail. Next photo, please, Andre."

Thirty minutes later, all the round thatched huts, tented

camps, game lodges, and hippo pools were beginning to run together. I closed my eyes. I was planning my weekend in my head when the sound of my name attracted my full attention.

The lights were back up and everyone was staring at me, obviously waiting for me to say something.

"Excuse me, Mr. Silverstein," I managed, "I'm afraid I didn't quite get that. Could you repeat it, please?"

"Of course, Sidney, of course," he said, his voice a deep rumble, "and I don't blame you for being flattered and completely overwhelmed, my dear. After all, it's not every day that one has the honor of being personally chosen—by me no less—to lead the very first group from Itchy Feet Travel ever to set foot on African soil."

What? Oh, dear Lord, I thought, *dear Lord, not me! Why me? Leading old ladies on safari? What have I done to deserve this?*

"I can't emphasize enough," he continued, oblivious to my stricken face and the short bursts of smothered laughter coming from Jay's corner, "how big this is going to be for our agency. Really, really big. Times are hard and I have decided that something like this is just what we need to get people traveling again, and more importantly, traveling with *us*. We are investing significant capital in this venture and failure is not an option. So it goes without saying that we must all get behind it and push, push, push! I want you all to understand, particularly you, Sidney, that our first trip out must be flawless. Do you hear me? Flawless."

"Flawless," Andre repeated.

Silverstein stared through his big glasses into the back corner of the room, focusing on Jay.

"And you, Jay Wilson, you lucky duck, will be assisting Sidney in escorting the very first safari group ever from Itchy Feet Travel. We will be offering our clients a deluxe ten-day tour to Cape Town, South Africa, including a safari at a private game lodge near the world-famous Kruger National Park. Did I mention that there will be no slipups? No slipups.

I want this first trip to be perfect. Do I make myself clear?"

I nodded.

The lucky duck nodded.

We all nodded.

Diana glared at me. She must have thought I was smirking, and I was, but not at her. No, my happy little smile was an expression of satisfaction because the gleeful snorting from the back corner had ended abruptly when Jay's name had been mentioned as the other tour escort.

Escorting a group of any age to Africa would be challenging. But Jay and I don't usually escort just any group. Our specialty is senior citizens, and escorting them is never exactly a breeze, even on a simple trip such as New England leaf-peeping. Some seniors are not in such great shape. Stuff happens. Guiding our agency's main senior group, the High Steppers, on a first-time safari in Africa would be a nightmare.

Nothing but silence from the back corner. Jay's heart had probably stopped.

"I would like to remind Sidney and Jay," Diana said, acid dripping from every word, "that there must be no repeat of their last trip, when several of our clients turned up dead."

Mr. Silverstein didn't like the interruption. "That will do, Diana," he said, waving her into a chair. "Everyone here knows what happened on that ill-fated cruise. The authorities have dealt with it and that case is closed. Today is not the time to bring that back up. We have exciting news to share here today."

"Exciting news, really exciting," Andre said.

Diana sat, eyes narrowed, her mouth in a thin line.

"Sidney," Mr. Silverstein said, beaming back at me, "in preparation for this product launch we are sending you and Jay on a fam trip next Wednesday. The fam will be hosted by the hotels, the inbound tour company, and the game lodge we are using for our tours."

My ears perked up at the words "fam trip." That got my full attention. Fam is short for familiarization. On a fam trip an agent is sent to check out a destination so he or she will know how to sell it. There are no clients on a fam trip, only a group of agents. Fam means a little education and a lot of fun. I shot a glance at Jay. He was smiling again.

"I want you to experience firsthand everything that we will be offering our clients long before any of them arrive in Africa. That way you can sort out in advance any problems that might occur with our arrangements. As I said earlier, on this first-ever African safari offered by Itchy Feet Travel there will be no problems, no slipups, no mistakes."

"No mistakes," Andre repeated.

Silverstein leaned over the podium, staring me down.

"It is your job, Sidney, to anticipate problems and solve them in advance. Do I make myself perfectly clear?"

I nodded.

"Jay?"

The steely eyes focused on him.

Jay nodded.

"And please remember, both of you, that I will hold you personally responsible for any glitches that are not resolved. Got it?"

Silverstein gave us each another piercing stare.

We both nodded.

"Then check your shot records and passports," he finished, "because you are leaving Kennedy next week on a direct flight to Cape Town."

I couldn't believe it. What great news. A fam trip! Not just any fam trip, a deluxe trip to South Africa. Not even the specter of the inevitable old folks' safari to follow could dim the joy of that moment. I mean, I was not just surprised, I was blown away.

You see, travel agents may be a dying breed. Very few of us survived after the pencil pushers and big financial wizards at the airlines decided to cut us out of the pie, effectively killing off their huge, nationwide, non-salaried sales force. I'm no MBA, but that seemed pretty dumb to me. But for those few of us left standing, stuff like fam trips is what keeps us in the biz.

Back in the day, great perks were the norm. Free passes to airline clubs, free drink coupons, comp tickets and upgrades, invitations to cocktail parties, dinners, and breakfasts ... not anymore. Those little goodies are now the stuff of legend for the frontline agent. Even the fam trip is sadly diminished. Times have changed. The sweet life is over. Now you usually pay a reduced-rate for pared-down fam trips and those remain only because agencies and suppliers have to do some boots-on-the-ground education in order to sell the product.

Familiarization is key. It is important for the travel agent to experience the product firsthand in order to better advise the customer, or better still, so he or she can recruit or escort a tour group to the destination. Photographs can lie. There really is no substitute—no brochure, no computer, no video—that does the job of the fam trip. But they are nowhere near as common as they used to be. And a really luxurious, amazing, all-expense paid fam to an exotic destination is rare indeed.

That bad feeling from outside the subway was wrong. Not bad news, good news! I had just been picked for a fam trip.

A terrific fam trip ...
With Jay!
To South Africa.
How lucky was that?

2

Nine days and a bruising twenty-two-hour plane ride later, Jay and I landed at Cape Town International Airport.

We got fifty dollars worth of South African rand out of an ATM and headed through the crowded airport, looking for our host and the van that would take us to the Commodore Hotel at the Victoria and Albert Waterfront in beautiful, beautiful Cape Town.

Jay thought he was way cool in his white pants, pink linen Armani shirt, and matching white linen Armani blazer, clearly his idea of tropical cosmopolitan chic. I had no idea if the pants were Armani, too. I suspected they were but wasn't about to ask.

Jay had actually changed clothes in the restroom on the plane just before we landed. I imagined his large frame cramped into that tiny bathroom stall, tugging on those tight pants. Unbelievable! Needless to say, Jay loves to dress up.

"Jealous," he sniffed, when he caught me smiling at his splendor, "just jealous, aren't you, Little Miss Polyester Princess?"

I ignored that. I'm used to Jay's digs about my wardrobe. It's not all polyester, but it doesn't cost my whole paycheck, either. That's for sure.

Jay is not just a travel agent and a co-worker, he is also my best friend, so I know him about as well as anyone can. There are some things he keeps private, of course, like his age. I'm twenty-seven, and I think he's ten or eleven years older, but I'll never be sure because he'll never tell. He prefers to be called Jay—he says because it rhymes with 'gay'—but his full name is Jeremiah Parker Wilson II. He was named for his stern and, fortunately, long-dead grandfather.

Grandfather Wilson was a devout Quaker and he must be constantly rolling in his grave over Jay's antics. Grandpa wanted Jay to stay home in Pennsylvania, marry a sweet little wife, raise a bunch of kids, and run the family dry-cleaning business. That wasn't happening. The minute they closed the lid on Grandpa, Jay was out of there, headed for New York.

Jay has been in this crazy travel business far longer than I have. His wardrobe is much nicer, and his apartment makes mine look like a room at the Y. He's physically powerful from his dedication to his gym. He's sharp, too; not much escapes either him or his wit. His physical fitness is a plus in escorting tour groups to odd places around the world. At 6'2" and over 200 pounds, Jay has gotten us out of some bad situations by his sheer bulk.

Jay has warm brown eyes, wild red hair, and a Van Dyke beard. The old ladies on our escorted tours adore him, and I do, too, although I'd swim the Hudson before admitting it. We work great together, and are paired on most trips.

"Halloooo! I say, Miss Marsh, Mr. Wilson. Hallooo!"

Near the exit, a tall, mustached man from our host tour company was energetically waving a sign bearing our names.

"Right-o," he said after we introduced ourselves, "my name is David. Follow me, please, our car is waiting."

David led us through the crowd toward the exit. His brown hair was cut short and beginning to thin on top. Perhaps that's why he compensated with the big mustache. He wore an ascot inside his linen shirt and a blue blazer with brass buttons and gray striped pants. At the curb, he chattered away in a pronounced British accent as the driver loaded our luggage into the hotel van and opened the doors so we could climb in. Jay and I were apparently the only agents from the fam tour arriving on our particular flight.

"The hotel is about twenty-five kilometers from the airport," David said, as we pulled away from the terminal, twisting around in the front seat to peer at us over his half-glasses. "Some members of our group arrived ahead of you and are already at the hotel." He glanced at his clipboard. "The rest are scheduled to arrive later today and at different times on various airlines throughout the evening, what?"

He gave us information packets, name badges and some truly awful safari hats.

Jay immediately put his on and winked at me. "What do you think, Sidney? African Queen?"

David looked offended by the interruption. He spoke directly to me, ignoring Jay.

"We'll just pop by the registration desk, my dear Miss Marsh, if you don't mind. After a welcoming cocktail party on The Terrace at six o'clock, your evening is free. You're on your own for dinner. The entire group will assemble bright and early in the morning for a breakfast seminar in the Blue Ribbon Room. Eight o'clock sharp."

"Thank you," I said. "That sounds lovely."

David nodded, then faced forward and, in his distinctive clipped speech, began a nonstop narrative about the buildings we were passing on the road into the city center.

The warm sunlight beaming through the windows welcomed us to Cape Town. Cape Town is second to Johannesburg in population, but first by far in beauty. Her history and location make her a melting pot for different cultures. Dominated by the stunning backdrop of Table Mountain and the sea, Cape Town has a wealth of architectural styles—Cape Dutch, elegant Victorian, Malay and Italian Renaissance—that blend beautifully with soaring modern design. Add to that the abundant tropical foliage, flowers, and trees, and Cape Town gets my vote for one of this planet's most beautiful cities.

David's narrative stopped as we neared the hotel. He gathered his papers and looked again at his clipboard.

"Except for tonight's dinner," he said, "all your meals and beverages will be complimentary. There's our hotel, just ahead. Welcome to Cape Town!"

Jay high-fived me, but David didn't see him.

⋇

Two agents from California had arrived just ahead of us and were sipping pink welcome drinks near the front desk as we entered the lobby. Jay popped his collar and headed straight for them and the free drinks while I signed us in at the desk and collected our key cards.

A stick-thin travel agent with pinched features, round wire-rims and straight red hair was holding up the line at the registration desk. Forty to forty-five, I guessed. She was insisting on speaking with the hotel manager, leaning over the desk, and waving her skinny arms. She was displeased with her room assignment and demanding an upgrade in a strident, shrill voice. Her printed name tag identified her as Mabel, and she was one of our group.

Finishing the paperwork, I turned away from the desk and rolled my carry-on toward the welcome table. There were goody bags and brochures laid out for us, and lots of pink drinks. After shaking hands with Jay's new friends, Chase and Rich, I gave Jay his key card and a duplicate of mine. I kept the extra one to his room. We always do that on trips. It comes in handy. I left him preening in the lobby while I headed for the elevator and a bath.

I'm not antisocial, but having slept in my clothes, I just wasn't set on sparkle.

⋇

One long and blissful shower later, and I was ready for Cape Town.

My hotel room was filled with light provided by high ceilings, tall windows, and French doors that opened onto a little balcony. The view of Table Mountain to my right and the harbor on my left was amazing.

Big commercial ships chugged past tour boats, fishing vessels, and elegant private yachts on the water below. Ships' horns sounded, piercing the cacophony of the market bustle. The breeze carried shouts of laughter, calls in multiple languages, and the tantalizing aromas of spices from the kitchens of restaurants lining the quay. African, French, Belgian, Indian, Thai, Chinese, Italian—Cape Town had it all.

My hotel was among several located at the Victoria and Albert Waterfront, which is a multibillion-rand commercial, shopping, and entertainment complex that faces a working harbor and dry dock. From my balcony I had a great view of the lively scene.

In addition to hotels, restaurants and shops, the V&A Waterfront features a large indoor craft market, Two Oceans Aquarium, and a maritime museum. I wanted to do it all, and thought how lucky a small-town Mississippi girl like me was to be here, on the very tip of Africa.

I was standing on the balcony in the fluffy hotel robe taking photos of the Waterfront when Jay entered the room with my spare key card, bearing two glasses and a bottle of Pinotage—South Africa's signature wine.

"To Cape Town, Sidney," he said as he filled my glass, "and to Sol Silverstein and all the poor shmucks back at Itchy who are slogging through a cold rain to work right about now. Doesn't that warm breeze feel terrific?"

"It sure does," I said, appreciating the wine's aroma. "That's the great thing about coming to the Southern Hemisphere in the fall. While it's getting colder at home, it's warming up here."

Jay clinked his glass with mine and leaned against the railing, watching the last rays of the sun cast an orange glow over the vibrant scene as it transitioned from late afternoon into evening. The market stalls were beginning to shut down for the night and boats were tying up. Candles were being lit on the tables of the sidewalk cafés.

"I love this place, Jay. I feel so lucky to be here. Isn't this room lovely? It couldn't be nicer."

"Yes, it could. George—that short guy with the red glasses in the check-in line ahead of us—took the room you were given on the room assignment list. He grabbed your corner room. It's bigger than this one."

"What? Some guy took my room? Why?"

"I don't know. He always wants the best, I think. I expect he heard that Mabel woman yelling about needing an upgrade and decided he would demand one, too. So he got the upgraded one and you got the standard. At least, that's what those two California guys told me. They said they heard it all when they were standing by the desk, just before we walked in. They pay attention to that sort of stuff. The desk clerk switched the rooms at this George guy's request."

"Well, that's fine with me. I don't care. I like this one. I don't think the other room could be much nicer. I feel so relaxed and pampered."

"You should be ready to roll tonight, Sidney, after all the sleep you got on the flight. How did you do that? I only slept in snatches."

"I took this magic little sleeping pill I got from my doctor along with my malaria pills, Jay. I wasn't sure if it would work, but it really did."

"No kidding. I thought about checking your pulse. You looked like you were dead. You were out for all the meals and movies and everything."

"True, and now I am starving. The welcoming cocktail party is at seven, but we're on our own after that. What do you think about grabbing a cab to the Mount Nelson Hotel for dinner? You know how I love grand old hotels, and even though I might never get to stay there, I would really love to see it."

"Sounds good to me, sweetie. I'll shower and shave and meet you downstairs. Try not to wear anything too tacky. You never know. The Mount Nelson is a pretty special place. We might meet someone famous."

When he was gone, I finished my wine and tore my attention away from the glorious view to the depressing sight of my closet.

Travel agents' salaries barely cover the rent in New York, leaving little extra for smashing little evening frocks. I was unprepared for the sophistication of Cape Town, having focused more on the safari portion of the trip, so my stuff was pretty utilitarian. Two dresses hung in my closet—one very casual and the other only slightly dressier.

It's always a good idea to read up thoroughly on a destination before you go, and review your itinerary before you pack. I usually do, but this trip had been unusually rushed. I thought Cape Town would be more like Nairobi. I was wrong. This is one reason why fam trips are so useful. Because of this trip, there would be no surprises for the High Steppers when we eventually brought them here. My old biddies aren't fond of surprises.

I pulled out my one slinky dress and a pair of black high-heeled sandals. I'm taller than average—5'8"—and slender; I wear a size six dress. In high heels I tower over most guys, so I brought flats, too, despite my love for stilettos. I decided against my cute red sundress, thinking that it was nowhere near elegant enough for an evening at the Mount Nelson.

The standard evening outfit I had brought was pretty simple, but it was my only choice. There would be no time in our crowded schedule for major shopping, either. That was unfortunate, because I clearly could have used another dress. Plus, I love to shop—a trait inherited from my Southern mother.

If our evenings ended up being as cosmopolitan as I suspected after our quick ride through this beautiful city, I knew I would be wearing that little black dress a lot before heading back to New York. Pack light, I preach to my clients. Pack light! Pack light! This time I thought I might have packed a little *too* light.

At least it's black, I thought, maybe I can buy some beads and stuff at the Greenmarket tomorrow to kick it up.

I brushed out my long black hair, pulled it up into a twist and added super-long silver earrings. Makeup for me is not a big deal. I have big, stormy gray eyes with long lashes, and if I do too much to them, I end up looking like the Bride of Dracula. I blotted my lipstick, locked the balcony and room doors, and headed downstairs.

Jay was at the bar with two other people we had briefly met in the lobby on arrival: George, the room thief, who was a short, wide travel agent from Sarasota, and Connie, a blonde from Atlanta. Connie was big and her husky laugh was even bigger. I liked her immediately. I could tell she was going to be a lot of fun. She was adorned with all kinds of bling, including flashy diamonds on every finger, and covered in hot pink and black zebra print.

George wore huge, red-framed glasses. His short brown hair was gelled into spikes or tufts that combined with his wide shoulders and short, square body to give him the look of a jolly owl. The owl impression was further enhanced by the constant motion of his head as it swiveled back and forth so as not to miss any new arrivals.

"Sweetheart! Great to see you again. Give Georgie-baby a kiss," he shrieked as he linked his arm in mine and steered me around the room, introducing me to the others. George had apparently already made friends with pretty much the whole group.

"Please. Is he running for mayor?" Jay said, after I finally managed to disentangle myself from George by declaring my need for a fresh drink. "You meet the guy once in the lobby and he's your new best friend." He looked around the room. "This thing is winding down, Sidney. Let's get out of here before he latches on to you again."

We jumped into a cab and headed for the Nellie, just as the great red sun slipped behind the mountain.

3

As our ratty old cab pulled up at the grand entrance of the brilliantly lit hotel, Jay pointed to the Bentley in front of us and said, "Now that is really more my style."

The Mount Nelson Hotel is a giant pink and white pile of colonial splendor sprawled across the lower slopes of Table Mountain and flanked by stately palm trees and lush gardens.

The cab had whizzed us from the Waterfront to the front door of the Nellie, speeding through the warm, flower-scented evening, from Adderley Street, up Government Avenue, past the Houses of Parliament through the center of one of the oldest sites of the original colony, the Company's Garden. This was the site of Jan van Riebeeck's huge vegetable garden, which he planted for the colony he founded in 1652 to provide fresh food for ships rounding the Cape of Good Hope. Now it is a lovely, peaceful area of exotic plants and trees for the city's residents and visitors. Museums, St. George's Cathedral and other historic buildings line its borders, much like our own National Mall.

Jay hopped out of—and quickly away from—the shabby cab. I knew from previous experience that he was pretending we had arrived in the Bentley and was hoping others might think so too. I followed him into the crowded lobby.

Our dinner reservations were at eight, and we were seated right away in the Planet Restaurant. The tables were candlelit. I loved the tall ceilings and big mirrors, reflecting star-like chandeliers.

"Nice," Jay said, as he scanned the faces of the other

diners before opening his menu. "Super nice. And looks like we've got a bonus, Sidney. Did you check out the prices?"

I looked at my menu. He was right. The setting was fantastic but the prices were the best surprise. They were a fraction of what they would have been in any comparable New York restaurant.

Jay chose the springbok loin. I had the poached king klip, a delicious native white fish. We shared a passion fruit soufflé for dessert. Because of the miracle of the exchange rate, the whole deal, with wine, set us each back about twenty-five bucks total.

Finally finished with the delicious dinner, we decided to head to the adjoining Planet Bar to enjoy an after-dinner drink.

"Get a champagne and try to look bored and world-weary," he whispered as we entered. "Work the room. I'm going to check out the terrace. See you later."

It was one of Jay's favorite games: we would act as though we were some kind of minor royalty—jaded sophisticates, Lord and Lady Something-or-Other—but our true aim was to spot an A-lister.

"Keep your eyes open, Sid," he said in a low voice as he moved away, "there's no telling who you might see here. This place is celebrity central."

There were plenty of glamorous-looking people in the room that night, but I guessed that many of them were imposters like me and Jay, more likely from Peoria than Paris. He disappeared through the tall doors onto the terrace. I was waiting at the bar for my drink before joining him when I heard someone call my name.

"Sidney, darling, what brings you to Africa?"

I turned to find Brooke Shyler, my one truly glamorous friend and sometime-client from New York. Brooke is in her late seventies or early eighties, though no one knows for sure. She doesn't look it and certainly isn't sharing that information. Brooke lives in an East Side penthouse, has heaps of money, and knows everyone interesting in the City. She is slender and always beautifully dressed, and her hair is even redder than Jay's.

"Brooke! How wonderful to see you. This is amazing. What on earth are you doing here? Jay and I are here on a fam trip for the agency, checking out a new tour. But what about you? What brings you to Cape Town?"

"Well, you know, darling, it's really cold and dreary in New York right now, and it's all warm and lovely here. So I decided to slip on over for a few weeks to soak up some sun. After I leave Cape Town on the twentieth, I'll be cruising with friends to the Seychelles and on to India. I'll be on a very special Empress Lines ship, Sidney, *The Rapture of the Deep*. Remember that ship? I wonder who the captain might be this time."

Her beautiful blue eyes sparkled. She loves to tease me about a certain ship's captain. That last cruise hadn't been all bad, for it had resulted in quite a passionate relationship with one Captain Stephanos Vargos.

"I don't know, Brooke. I haven't heard from any ship captains lately. I don't know what assignments he's drawn. Things were a little rocky between us the last time he was in New York."

"Really? Let me guess. He's ready to take you to Athens for good and you are not ready to commit."

"Something like that."

"Well, the captain of this particular cruise could turn out to be short, fat, and ugly, I suppose, but if he is a tall, handsome Greek, I'll be sure that he knows you are in the neighborhood, darling. The ship will dock here on the nineteenth."

She smiled, but her eyes were serious.

"I wouldn't let that one slip through my fingers, Sidney. Men like that don't come around very often. Now come and meet my friends."

Brooke has many, many friends all over the world, and they range from movie stars and tycoons to ordinary people like me. As I said, she is an amazing woman.

♓

I had such a good time with Brooke and her pals that I lost track of time … and of Jay. When I realized how late it was, I said my goodbyes and started looking for him.

I didn't see him in the bar, or on the terrace, but someone said he might be in the garden, so I went down the steps into the fragrant, moonlit night to find him. The enormous ivory globe of the African moon rose over the trees and flooded the path with light. That moon made the discreet pathway lights, thoughtfully placed by the garden's designers, almost unnecessary. The moon was as yet only half full, but it shone brightly. I could only imagine how beautiful it would be in the nights to come.

I looked down one empty path, and then another, and saw three men beneath the trees at the far end with their backs turned, deep in conversation.

It was too dark to tell at a distance if one of them was Jay or not, but one guy was about Jay's height and the white pants he wore stood out against the dark shrubbery. The other men were short and stocky, like George, wearing dark clothing. One of the short men left the group, striding away out of sight, into the trees. I started down the path toward the two who remained, smiling and waving, thinking that it had to be Jay. No one else in the bar had been dressed like Clark Gable in the John Ford classic, *Mogambo*.

From the looks of it, the two men seemed to be having an argument, though they were speaking in low tones and I couldn't hear what they were saying. I was just a few feet away when they stopped talking and turned to stare at me.

Pretty embarrassing.

It was not Jay. I had never seen either of them before. The great-looking man in the white pants was Jay's height, with shoulders just as broad. His hair was dark instead of red and much longer, brushing the collar of his dark coat. His strong jaw, unlike Jay's, was clean-shaven. Even in the darkness, I could see that his handsome face was contorted in rage. His companion was a short, sturdy black man, with powerful shoulders and a grim expression. He wore an expensive dark suit and a large diamond ring.

Their reaction to my arrival was odd. Each man just stared, then turned abruptly and walked quickly away from me and from each other, in opposite directions, without another word.

I just stood there in the moonlight. Jay was nowhere in sight.

I shivered. I was alone in the lush, tropical garden. There were no sounds except for the faint melody of a piano coming from the hotel and the crunch of gravel receding as the two men retreated.

The moon drifted behind some clouds, making the night even darker, and the deep shadows of the overhanging trees suddenly made me feel very lonely indeed.

I hurried back toward the hotel, getting pebbles in my sandals, but I definitely wasn't stopping in the deserted garden to empty them.

In my haste, I tripped over something, a broken tree limb, maybe, and went sprawling. I didn't investigate. I jumped up, brushed myself off, and jogged off as fast as I could go toward light and people. My dress was okay and I wasn't hurt, just shaken.

As I neared the hotel, I was glad to see George, leaning on a railing, smoking a cigar.

"Hello, Sidney. Isn't this a great hotel? Don't you wish you could just check in here for a year or two and paint or something?"

"Yes, I do," I laughed, "but my budget won't allow one night, much less a couple of years. What are you doing here, George? I thought you were going to a disco."

"Changed my mind when I heard you and Jay had headed here. Thought I might as well have a look. I'm glad I did. This place is impressive."

"It is, isn't it?"

"Where's Jay? Why isn't he with you? Were you out in the garden all by yourself?"

I wasn't about to tell George about my embarrassing encounter with two strange men in the garden.

"Yes," I said, trying to quell the faint tremor in my voice. "I just strolled out from the bar for a moment to get some fresh air." I thought back to the men in the shadows of the deserted garden. I couldn't quite shake the notion that I had seen something clandestine. Maybe it was that look of rage in the face of the handsome man ...

"It's really beautiful, isn't it? See anyone you know in the garden? Did you take any pictures?"

I shrugged and held up my hands to show that they were empty. "No, and I didn't bring my camera with me tonight. Travelling light. I'm not sure how well pictures would turn out, in any case. Low light, you know."

"Yeah, depends on how good the camera is, I guess. Where's Jay? Did he go in the garden?"

"I think Jay's inside. It's getting late." I started walking toward the hotel. "I better find him, grab a cab, and head back to the Waterfront. Want to share a ride?"

"No, thanks. I haven't been here long. I think I'll stay awhile. Good night, Sidney."

He turned back, facing the steps, puffing on the cigar.

"Good night, then, George," I called, "See you in the morning."

I had just stepped into the bar when I saw Jay, the real Jay this time. There was no mistaking that red hair in the

23

lights of the bar. In the dark, all colors just wash out.

"Jay! I'm so glad to find you. I've been looking all over the place. I almost grabbed a perfect stranger out there in the bushes because I thought it was you. Then I ran into George, who asked about a million questions about it. He has so much curiosity, maybe even more than I have."

Jay smiled down at me. "No one has more than you, Sidney."

I sat down on a chair to fish the pebbles out of my shoes, shaking my head at how many I had managed to accumulate. "I walked all over that garden looking for you, Jay. I did a little dance, too, when I tripped over something on the path. I almost fell on my face."

"Well, I've been looking for you, too, babe, because that plane ride from hell is beginning to catch up with me. I hate to admit it, sweetie, but Big Jay is tired." He stifled a yawn. "What do you think? Have you had enough fun? You look like you have." He brushed a stray lock of hair back from my face. "Were you dancing? Your crowning glory is a mess."

"I told you I tripped over something and fell in the garden," I said. I pulled the remaining pins out of my hair and shook it out, letting it fall loose onto my shoulders.

"You okay, Sid?" He stared at me. "You're not hurt, are you?"

"No, but I am also ready to go back to the Commodore. You're so right. It's late, and we have to be at David's breakfast seminar in a few hours."

We walked down the steps and climbed into a waiting cab.

"Did you see Brooke?" I asked Jay, as we rolled away into the fragrant night. "How funny to run into her here, halfway around the world."

"Yes, I did," he said, leaning back on the lumpy old car seat, his eyes half-closed. "She told me how she just decided to pop over and grab some sun. Now wouldn't that be nice?

Don't you wish you could do that? Just go wherever you want, whenever you want? I think she should adopt me, Sidney. You can adopt adults, you know. Then I would never have to work again and I could live like that all the time. Why don't you speak to her about that idea, Sid, the next time you see her? Tell her she should adopt me. It's the least you could do for me, after all I've done for you."

I laughed. "Great idea, Jay. I'll get right on that."

Honestly. I couldn't believe the way Jay's mind worked. And the thing is, he was only half-kidding. He would let Brooke adopt him in a heartbeat and never look back.

I know Jay. He is my best friend. I know him well.

4

The next morning, over scrambled eggs, toast and marmalade, we met with our tour leader, David, and the rest of the group.

David was dressed in a white linen suit that looked as if he might just have a panama hat around somewhere to go with it. I'm sure Jay approved, and was more than a little envious. David brought a bundle of local newspapers, which he handed to George to pass around. George looked as if he had had an extremely late night. He must have stayed at the bar long after we left.

David tapped on the little podium with a pointer. "Ladies and gentlemen! Today we will be embarking on a *splendid adventure,* which promises *rare excitement* to all of our *thousands* of international visitors, but particularly to those of you right here in this room."

Along with lots of extra emphasis, David rolled the Rs on "rare" and "right" and "room."

"South Africa is a *captivating* land of *amazing* beauty with an *astonishing* variety of flora and fauna."

He tapped on the table with the pointer and then tucked it under his arm like a swagger stick.

"Now please direct your attention to the first of the brochures in the information packets I have prepared for you. We begin our adventure this morning with ..."

Jay passed me a note during the introductory speech:

Bleh. David claims to have a missus somewhere, but he is

gayer than I am, and he is not English, either. That accent is faker than my Rolex. He is probably from Jersey.

I had my own doubts about David's British authenticity, but I didn't care in the least. The itinerary he was describing sounded great, phony accent or no phony accent. I looked over the printed itinerary as he filled in the details.

The day's plan called for us to have a short presentation on Cape Town and South Africa, followed by a city tour, lunch included, and an afternoon boat ride to Robben Island, where Nelson Mandela was imprisoned for so many years. Then we would be driven back to the V&A Waterfront for dinner at a lovely Belgian restaurant called Den Anker.

On the next day's schedule was a tour to Cape Point and the Cape of Good Hope, then lunch with an afternoon tour of Simon's Town and Kirstenboch Gardens. The following morning we were scheduled for an early flight to a tiny airport at Hoedspruit, near our private game reserve on the edge of Kruger National Park. Drivers from our safari lodge would pick us up in Land Rovers at the little airport and drive us into the game reserve.

"After four days of *drrrrrinking in* the *magnificent* flora and fauna of the camp, some of you will return to Johannesburg and then onwards home. Others will have a tour extension, allowing additional time back here in Cape Town to see other sights and discuss business arrangements and future bookings."

Jay and I were booked for the extension. After the safari, we were scheduled to remain in Cape Town for a few days to meet with hotel people and other travel vendors. In those meetings we would finalize the specific venues and arrangements for the custom tour our agency was promoting.

We heard a lot of housekeeping details about the next day's departure, received thick packets of handouts and brochures, and viewed a video of different properties offered by David's company. Finally David dismissed us for a short break before the City Tour.

I stretched. "I'm going up to my room to dump all of this junk and get my camera, Jay. Need anything?"

"No, thanks," he said, stuffing a newspaper in his man-bag. "I'm going to get some more rand out of the ATM and grab some water. I'll meet you at the van."

⯎

The housekeeper's cart was at the door of my room as I came down the hall, and the door was partially open. I could hear someone rumbling around in the bathroom, apparently cleaning. I didn't linger, just dropped all the stuff on the desk, grabbed my camera, and headed back to the elevator.

I almost bumped into George, who was making a few selections from the maid's unattended cart.

"Ha! Caught you, George. Bet you didn't think anyone would see you pilfering."

He stiffened in self-righteous indignation. "I am not pilfering. This stuff is for the guests and I am a guest. Want some of this bath gel?"

"No, thanks," I laughed. "There's plenty in my room."

I caught the elevator back down, joined by George, whose pockets were bulging with maid-cart booty.

I saw only strangers in the lobby, so I walked straight through and out the front door to the parking area where the tour vans were waiting. George followed. Heading toward my assigned van, I jammed my key card into the back pocket of my shorts. Those shorts were beginning to get a little too tight ... too much great food already on this trip. Unfortunately they were all I had, and the day was predicted to be hot. I could feel the glances at my rear end, even from George. I ignored the suggestive comments I overheard from the bell stand.

It might seem strange that I did not carry a purse, but I gave up purses on trips some time ago. Huge purses look great, but they are also a huge pain. They just weigh you down and make you a target in sketchy situations. Also, people like Jay constantly give you stuff to carry for them.

"Here," he'll say, handing me some trophy he's snagged, "Just stick this in your purse." Eventually my bag would be overflowing with junk he didn't remember handing to me in the first place.

It didn't take me long to lose the purse habit and develop a new method. That was quite a change for me because girls in my hometown are born with purses in their hands. Southern women go all the way to their graves clutching handbags. Now, after years of lugging junk around, I am free. My serious money and stuff like passports and credit cards go in a neck purse under my shirt or in the room safe. My little walking around money goes in my pockets. That way, my hands are free and I'm less of a target for theft.

Outside in the bright morning sunlight of the hotel entrance, cars and trucks constantly arrived and departed. Motorcycles whizzed by, and people and luggage moved in and out in a sort of controlled confusion. We headed toward a line of vans from David's tour company waiting at the hotel entrance. Our group was already loading. I found my van and waved bye to George, who was assigned to a different one.

Jay was seated in front, next to the driver's seat, reading one of the local newspapers that David had distributed.

I climbed into the second row next to two sisters, Gwendolyn and Matilda, who were travel agents from a British agency in the Midlands and could almost have passed for twins. Both of them were middle-aged, round, and cheery, and had straight, short, blond-going-gray hairstyles, sturdy shoes, fanny packs, and blue eyes. They chattered nonstop to anyone who would listen, finishing each other's sentences.

"Why, hello, Sidney, it's so nice to meet you, please call me Wendy—"

"And I'm Tilda. We're from—"

"Birmingham. And you are from New—"

"York? We went there last year for the first time—"

"And we just loved it, didn't we, Tilda?"

"My yes, Wendy, and everything had such—"

"Energy! That's what we both noticed, wasn't it, darling?"

Giggling in agreement, the sisters beamed at me, blond heads bobbing.

"Check this out," Jay said, handing me the front page of the newspaper, folded in half.

" '*Body Found in Garden of Landmark Hotel*,' " I read.

"They found a dead guy right after we left last night," he murmured, "and after that, no one was allowed to enter or leave while they investigated. We were lucky to get out when we did, huh?"

"Yeah," I said, scanning the story.

"Oh, my goodness, Tilly, look at this!"

One of the sisters was leaning over me, reading the headline.

I was finished with the story so I handed the paper over to her. Its contents launched them into a frenzy of speculation.

I didn't hear a word. I was thinking back over the evening and my brief venture into that garden, wondering if I should call someone and describe the men I saw. "Jay—"

"Forget it, Sidney. I know what you are thinking, but you didn't really see anything. You just saw some guys talking. They could just as easily describe seeing you. Don't get involved. Don't call anyone. It could totally screw up our trip. Fugetaboudit, sweetie, unless you think that limb you tripped over was really a foot."

The thought made me shudder, but I decided he was right. I had little to add and even the smallest delay could keep me in Cape Town while the group left on safari.

"Give it a day, Sid. We'll watch the news. They don't

even know the cause of death yet. One day. It might be nothing but a heart attack. There's a reason for that saying, 'Don't borrow trouble.' Trouble seems to come your way even when you're not looking for it. Lay low, babe. Chill."

David poked his head into the van then, doing a head count. The sisters shoved the newspaper in his face, pelting him with questions. He said he didn't know anything about it, had nothing to add to the story.

I sat silently staring out the window, remembering the dark garden as the van rolled out of the parking lot, headed to Table Mountain. Jay was right. I hadn't seen much—just two men arguing.

Fortunately, the sights of the beautiful city quickly replaced the front page news in the British sisters' thoughts. They were soon squealing over the scenery instead of the newspaper, which was fine with me. Wendy and Tilda warbled on the entire morning, commenting on everything we passed, drowning out the guide. They gasped, exclaimed, giggled, and photographed anything and everything.

No one else said a word. They couldn't. I had to admire the sisters' enthusiasm, but Jay looked ready to pinch their heads off.

During introductions at the morning seminar, David had mentioned that on safari we would be traveling on daily game drives, morning and evening. We would travel in the Land Rovers in groups of seven or so, along with a driver and a game spotter. Each day we would be assigned to the same vehicle, with the same fellow passengers, and usually the same driver and spotter, for the entire safari.

That meant that if we stayed cooped up in the car for too long with Wendy and Tilda, the odds were good that we could get trapped with them for the entire trip. I didn't really mind. They were really very sweet, and their enthusiasm was endearing, but Jay didn't feel the same way. He was seriously annoyed.

By the time we reached the famous Table Mountain Aerial Cableway station and were able to bail out of that chattering van and get in line for the ride up the mountain, Jay and I realized that we had better get busy.

We needed to find some new friends.

5

We were in a glass-walled cable car halfway up magnificent Table Mountain, buffeted by a strong wind. Though commonly called a cable car, it looked actually like a giant blue gondola, suspended on thick steel cables. The revolving floor was designed so that no passenger would be cheated of the amazing view. All of Cape Town and Table Bay glittered far below.

When the strange hand brushed lightly across my rear end in the crowded compartment, it was not just there for a friendly pat. I'm not a bad-looking girl and I've ridden crowded buses and subways all over the world. Pats I know and understand.

This was a treasure hunter. A thief.

But I am not a newbie and my credit card was not in my back pocket. The pickpocket must have been pretty disappointed with the plastic hotel key card he stole instead.

I immediately turned around, searching the faces of the other passengers for clues, signs of guilt, but the perp was either a really good actor or had melted back into the crowd before I could spot him.

I didn't scream. It wouldn't do any good. I had been pick-pocketed once before in Athens on a jam-packed train. These petty thieves work worldwide in crowded subways, trains, and elevators. Like I said, I learned the hard way not to carry anything valuable in my back pockets.

"Jay," I said, louder than normal, "watch your back. I think someone just lifted my key card out of my back pocket."

"Really?" he said, also in a loud voice, looking behind him at the others. "A pickpocket? Well, here, Sidney, stand in front of me then. No one will mess with my pockets unless he wants his arm broken."

He looked down at me, his voice quieter, "They didn't get anything valuable, did they? I know you're careful with what you put in your pockets."

"No, they just got the key card and that little printed itinerary card that David gave us this morning. It doesn't really matter. Both are easily replaced, but I hate it."

"Of course you do, sweetie, and so do I, but don't let it ruin your day. Bet that dude is disappointed. Those tight shorts really showed off the outline of what he probably thought was a credit card. What did you pay for those shorts, anyway? Five bucks?"

"No, ten. Okay, okay, I got them on closeout. Maybe eight. Look, I know they're not designer like yours. I admit it. Don't make me feel bad about that, too."

"I'm not. I love you no matter how cheap your clothing is, Sidney. Tell you what. You figure out who did the pick-pocketing and I'll thump him, okay?"

I had to smile at that. That's one of the great things about Jay. He is totally perceptive and he has this people magic. He knows exactly how to use his wit to make the best of a bad situation.

Whatever. The key card was gone forever. It was not a big deal, just invasive and annoying. Jay would give me his extra one, or I could get another at the front desk.

I wondered if Tilda might have captured the incident and the thief with her camera. She was right behind me on my left when it happened, and she was constantly snapping away at everything and everyone. I looked around for her, but she had apparently moved to the other side of the car. I didn't want to shout, so I decided to quiz her after we unloaded at the top of the mountain.

There was also the slight possibility that the card had fallen out of my pocket earlier. I had taken the little itinerary card out for a look while we were waiting in line to board. Maybe I had unknowingly pulled the key card out along with it, and then dropped it. The touch I felt might have been a creep after all instead of a thief. But I didn't think so. The itinerary card was gone too. I was pretty sure both items had been lifted.

Whatever. It could have been much worse.

No one else seemed to have noticed my tiny drama. Why would they, with this view?

People jammed against the windows, our group and a bunch of other tourists, all taking photos, admiring the scenery. Everyone gasped whenever a gust of wind swayed the cable car.

The view of Cape Town below, the mountain, the sun sparkling on the sea, the ride alone took my breath away. The loss of a key card certainly couldn't spoil the thrill.

We were in the shadow of the mountaintop when the power failed. The lights went out, the floor stopped revolving, and we all screamed before falling silent.

Now the only sound was the whistle of the wind and the creaking of the cable.

I looked out the window at the ground, thousands of feet below.

Jay reached for my hand and gave it a little squeeze. I don't do heights well, and he knows it. I'm not a big fan of vehicles that revolve, either.

The lights flickered twice, the mechanism started grinding, and the power came back on.

We began to revolve again and in a moment we were at the top of the mountain. Relief flowed through me and apparently everyone else, too, evident in all of the bad jokes and nervous laughter that rolled through the crowd after we made it to the top. Even the strangers among us were swept up in a camaraderie sparked by shared terror.

"I swear I just about wet my pants," said Connie.

"Pip, pip," chirped a cruise agent from Liverpool, "I say, that was almost as thrilling as being in one of those huge round bars atop a Cunard ship in a storm, what?"

My ears perked up at that. This guy really had no idea what he was talking about. What a phony. Everyone familiar with the cruise business knows that those high round bars are a signature feature of Royal Caribbean Cruise Line ships. RCCL, but not Cunard.

How could this guy call himself a travel agent? A cruise agent? A British cruise agent? He had either misspoken or he was the worst travel agent in England.

Or he was simply weird. He was humming and chuckling to himself, rocking back on his heels. He whistled softly through the gap in his big front teeth, apparently believing that he had said something very clever. Peering through the window, he shaded his tiny pig's eyes with meaty freckled hands. A long-billed cap was jammed onto his head with a few wisps of ginger hair escaping on the sides. A flap hanging from the back edge of the cap covered most of his thick neck. A rumpled safari shirt stretched across his belly, and his pants were the kind that zip off at the knee. He looked like a butcher on holiday, not a travel agent. His name tag said "Hello! My name is Dennis."

The cable car slid to a stop and the doors opened. We stepped out onto the platform, and I forgot all about the stolen key card, the balky engine, and Dennis.

I was blown away by the view.

Table Mountain is easily the most recognizable natural feature of South Africa. It is a giant, flat-topped granite, shale, and sandstone slab that dominates Cape Town. It is visible to ships over ninety miles out to sea. Ancient sailors must have been awed by it as well, for geologists say that the massive landmark rose from the sea some 250 million years ago.

David said that we were lucky to have such a clear day, for the mountain can often be suddenly shrouded in a thick white mist that locals call "the tablecloth." He spoke of a legend about the mist being caused by a smoking contest between a Dutchman and the Devil. Because of the legend, the peak where the clouds begin to form is called "Devil's Peak."

After everyone had taken all the photos they wanted and fully admired the view, I finally got a chance to mention the pickpocket to Tilda. After a lot of clucking, she kindly checked her camera memory for an image. Nothing significant showed up. By then I regretted mentioning it at all, with all the fuss Tilda and Wendy were making.

David announced a short break. Most of the group headed for the restrooms and the coffee and gift shops, with Tilda and Wendy in the lead. Dennis was chatting up some boys selling souvenirs.

Checking my camera battery, I started down a boulder-lined path toward the edge of the mountain. I wanted good photos of the mountain called Lion's Head and the famous Devil's Peak, and of Table Bay, glowing azure blue far below us. Photos taken while on a fam trip are invaluable when it comes time to actually sell the trip to clients. With the pictures downloaded to my laptop, I'd be able to show them what they would personally experience while on their vacation.

"Where are you going, Sidney?" Jay called out. "The shop is this way. Don't you want coffee and a pastry?"

"I'll grab something later. Right now I just want to get some good shots of this magnificent view."

"Well, don't get near the edge, sweetie," he laughed. "I'd hate for your little ass to fall right off the Table. And you watch out on those lonely paths, too. Remember the pickpocket, and what the driver said in the van about the bad guys."

I nodded and waved before walking against the wind toward the precipice. Soon all thoughts of schedules, sketchy people and dire warnings were shoved aside by the awe of what I was seeing.

We had received multiple warnings from the van driver and David that the more isolated areas of Table Mountain were prime places for muggings, particularly of unsuspecting tourists. But that day, the only creatures hiding in the rocks were the dassies, or rock hyraxes—ancient little mammals that share an ancestry with the elephant.

They don't look like elephants, I thought, more like big, fat guinea pigs.

The dassies basked in the sun, their cute little eyes closed, the wind ruffling their light brown fur. One alert little fellow stood sentry, anxiously peering around. I stepped off the path into the rocks, bent over, and crouched down, silently creeping closer to the little creatures, focusing my lens, hoping for a good shot.

A shadow passed over the sun, and the sentry dassie sounded a high-pitched bark of alarm, sending them all scurrying away. I was left alone, squatting among the rocks.

Well, not quite alone.

A tall Afrikaner stood smiling down at me from the path, his white linen shirt ruffling in the breeze. His Dutch ancestry showed in his broad shoulders and strong face. That face seemed familiar, and at first I wondered if he could have been in the cable car with us, but I quickly realized that I would have noticed such a good-looking man.

He was tanned and handsome, with longish brown hair swept back from his face by the wind. He was clearly amused at the sight of me clambering up from the rocks, embarrassed at having been caught with my fanny up in the air.

"There. I've spoiled your shot. I'm sorry, darling, but perhaps you'll forgive me when you see where you almost trod."

I followed his gaze to a spot near where I had crouched, just in time to see a large Cape cobra slither away into the rocks.

I shrieked and jumped back onto the path, shuddering, careening into my new friend. He threw his arms around me to halt my headlong, hysterical flight. His broad shoulders shook with laughter.

"Still, now, love. It's quite all right. Be still. He's gone now, and you're quite safe here with me."

I looked up into his sharp green eyes and wondered for a moment if that were true. He released me and grinned as I tried to gather my wits and my scattered belongings.

Why, oh why, Sidney, do you always manage to look like such an utter fool whenever an attractive man crosses your path?

"I wouldn't go wandering about like that again, love, if I were you. As I suppose you now realize, there can be some rather bad things hidden among the rocks in this spectacular land."

"Thank you," I said, twisting my tangled black hair into a ponytail and securing it with a band. "You're quite right. I wasn't thinking. I guess I never have been very good at minding warnings."

We both looked at the signpost, which clearly forbid stepping from the path and warned of danger. It even had the outline of a snake drawn on it.

"Right, then," he said with a wide smile, "Now, how about joining me for a drink, to calm those nerves?"

That sounded great to me.

We were just going up the steps of the restaurant when Jay appeared. Of course. He had always had perfect timing.

"There you are, Sidney. Where in the hell have you been? I've been looking all over this mountain for you. We're going to be left. Everyone's waiting."

Crap.

Jay was right. I was late. The others were waiting. I could see them all standing impatiently on the platform, rightfully annoyed, staring daggers at me for being tardy. I had broken a cardinal rule of group travel: never keep the bus waiting.

I looked up at my new friend. "I guess we won't have that drink after all. I'm with a group. I have to go. Thanks for the offer and for helping me on the path."

"Anytime. I quite enjoyed rescuing you from the deadly serpent. Perhaps we'll see each other again before you leave Africa. What is your name, lady? And how long will you be at the Mount Nelson?"

Jay gave me a fierce look and started shaking his head. He grabbed my hand, just as it finally dawned on me where I had seen this man before. This was the guy I had mistaken for Jay in the moonlit garden at the Nellie. No wonder he seemed familiar. I tried to pull away from Jay but he had a firm grip on my arm and was marching me forward.

"I'm not at the Nellie," I called out over my shoulder. "But I'd love to have drinks sometime. I'm at the Commodore, at the Victoria and Albert Waterfront, and my name is Sidney." Jay was dragging me away toward the group. "Sidney Lanier Marsh." I hoped he would call. You just don't run into a guy like that every day.

We had twirled halfway back down the mountain when I realized that he had never told me *his* name.

Damn.

6

"Rule Number One," preached Jay, while on the ferry to Robben Island, "is that you don't shout out your name and hotel to strange, random men in a foreign country. Why don't you just scream out your room number, too, and your bra size while you're at it?"

"Rule Number Two," I retorted, "is 'Mind Your Own Business.' "

"Please. You need someone to mind your business for you, Sidney. Just when I think you are getting a little street smart, turning into a real New Yorker, you pull a dumb hick stunt like that. You saw this guy in the garden, in the dark, where the newspaper said that the stiff was found, right? So what if *he* is the perp?"

Ooooh. He was right, obviously. I tried to change the subject. "Okay, Jay, okay. You're right. I had a brain lapse. Let's just drop it for now. We're almost to the dock. Aren't you excited to be seeing Robben Island?"

"No. I'm not. Not when I had to give up my tour of wine country, with free tastings, to visit some grim old prison on a desolate island. I'm not big on history, Sidney, you know that."

Like I said earlier. Jay is a great guy, but sometimes his priorities are a little skewed.

✳

By nightfall, everyone was really tired and suffering from sensory overload.

"How could you not be moved by the sight of that jail cell?" demanded Rose Abrams, an agency owner from Miami, as we filed off the van for dinner at Den Anker.

"I'm just saying that another country's politics are NONE of our business," shouted Mabel Something-Or-Other, a totally unbearable mall agent from Iowa. She was the one I had seen at the hotel check-in, demanding a better room.

"Human rights are EVERYONE'S business," Rose shouted back.

"Go, go, go, Sidney," said Jay. "Keep moving, keep moving, move away from those two. I'm sick of them both. Find the bar. We'll get a table later, after they're seated. I'm not listening to any controversy over dinner."

"Well, at least admit Rose is right, Jay. You know she is."

"Of course she is, but I've heard just about all the arguing I can stand for one day. Let's get a drink. I want a Belgian beer."

"Okay, okay," I said, taking a seat at the bar, "but just so you know, I'm telling you that I like Rose a lot, but I can't take much more of Mabel. If she gets in our van tomorrow, I'm getting out. Wendy and Tilda are not a problem for me, but Mabel is. I mean it."

George and Connie joined us at the bar along with the two travel insurance reps from California, Chase and Rich, who said their home was in L.A. They introduced us all to Fernando, a tall, dark, and witty group tour representative for Alitalia. Fernando was based in Rome. We took an immediate liking to all of them, and everyone had the same idea that Jay and I had about finding a good group for the game drives, so it looked like we were set.

Chase and Rich were thirtyish, edgy, also tanned and fit, with highlighted blond hair. They had taken obvious care in their wardrobe selection for the evening. The cuffs of their crisp shirtsleeves were folded back just so to reveal expensive designer watches. The creases in their trousers were sharp. Nothing they wore looked as if it had come from a suitcase after a transatlantic flight. Our hotel was within walking distance of the restaurant. Chase and Rich had asked to be let off at the hotel to dress for dinner instead of going straight on to the restaurant from the tour like the rest of us. Jay's heart probably skipped a beat when he heard their request. Eager for a drink and a meal, he hadn't thought of changing.

Both of them might have just stepped out of an ad. They looked so much alike that it was difficult to keep them straight.

Chase was a little taller than Rich, and his eyes were brown instead of blue. I noticed one distinct difference between the two: Chase had a long ugly scar on the side of his neck that he said came from a childhood attack by a vicious dog. That traumatic encounter had left him deathly afraid of animals. He said Rich had had to convince him that it would be safe to go on safari.

"Don't feel bad about that, Chase," said Jay, sipping a mango martini. "I'm not nuts about wild animals, either. I want to call nine-one-one if I see so much as a rat in the subway. But I wasn't going to pass up a chance to go on safari. A safari is about as glamorous as it gets, don't you think? I expect the game lodge people will keep us all pretty safe. I hope so, anyway."

Jay was playing it super cool in front of the California agents, acting blasé about his genuine fear of wild animals. I knew the real story. He had voiced his concerns to me over coffee right after we got this assignment. Jay had considered turning Silverstein down, but he couldn't stand missing out on any fun. Plus, there was the glamour factor and the certainty of great stories that would fuel his cocktail conversation for years to come.

I could tell that Jay was intimidated by the splendor of the California agents' attire. Right after we ordered drinks, he excused himself and disappeared down a hallway. When he came back from the men's room, he had tousled his hair and popped his collar.

"Great look," I whispered, "love the collar."

"Shut up, just shut up. Your idea of a fashion statement is a hoopskirt."

He ignored me then, so I sat on the opposite side of the table next to Fernando Corelli, the Alitalia rep.

Fernando was tall and lean, but he was also muscular. I knew that he was quite strong, because I had watched him lift Wendy and Tilda's heavy suitcases with ease, as if they weighed nothing. He had short, curly dark hair and eyes with long lashes, classic Roman features, and a clever, sarcastic wit. He spoke very good English, but with a heavy Italian accent. He wore his European-cut clothing with that cool nonchalance that Jay constantly dreamed of attaining.

Fernando had a deep tan, as if he spent a lot of time working outdoors. That seemed kind of strange for an airline rep, but he told us he rode a bicycle to and from work every day, so maybe that explained it.

He was very amusing, particularly when recounting his description of his ferry ride over to Robben Island. He had become separated from our group, and had ridden over on the ferry sandwiched in with the members of a holiday group of South Africans in native dress from the Limpopo River region. They had apparently mistaken handsome Fernando for some soccer star, a misidentification that he relished and did not correct until the photo requests overwhelmed him.

"I confessed then that I was not who they thought I was, but it was no use. They were convinced that they were correct and that I was just lying. I thought I would never escape. That's why it took me so long to find you and rejoin the tour."

"People think I am a celebrity, too," said Jay. "Happens all the time."

Please.

I tried to meet his eyes, but he wouldn't look my way.

"Where is the Limpopo River, y'all?" Connie asked. "I swear I heard that name somewhere before. I don't know where. Limpopo. I like how it sounds. Lim-po-po."

"Think of Kipling, *tesore*," Fernando said. "Remember, '*The Elephant's Child*'? When his insatiable curiosity took him to 'the dark, grey-green, greasy Limpopo River, all set about with fever-trees ...' "

"Nah," Connie said. "I never saw it. Must not have made it to the Metroplex. Maybe it'll be on TV."

"Maybe," Fernando said, breaking into an easy smile.

H

After dinner, I strolled back along the Waterfront from the restaurant to the hotel with Fernando and George. The reflection of lights glimmered on the water. Commercial fishing boats and private yachts tied up along the piers creaked and rocked against their moorings on the outgoing tide. Strains of music mingled with conversation and laughter as people lingered over drinks and coffee in the candlelit, open-air cafés lining the pier.

Fernando, George, and I were calling it a night. Jay, Chase, Rich, and Connie had all declared that the evening was far from over. They announced that they were heading out to check out the clubs. Jay said I was a party pooper.

"Bye, y'all," Connie yelled from the cab window as they rolled away, "LIM-PO-PO!"

"I hope they get back okay," I said, as we watched them drive out of the bright lights of the Waterfront. The cab zoomed up a dark street, bound for the fabled Drum Café.

"I wouldn't worry, if I were you," said George. "This isn't Jo'burg. They should be safe enough."

"Did you hear the guards on Robben Island today talking about all the diamond smuggling, kidnappings, poaching, and drug trade in Johannesburg and at the border of Zimbabwe?" I asked. "I wanted to ask more about it, but David was rushing us along. Aren't we going to Johannesburg tomorrow?"

"Yes," George answered, "but only to change planes. We will never leave the airport."

"But when we are in safari camp, near Kruger, Sidney," Fernando said, "we won't be too far from the borders of Mozambique and Zimbabwe. The northern border of Kruger really does lie along that 'great, grey-green, greasy Limpopo River.' Cross the river to the north, and you're in Zimbabwe. A few miles to the east, and it's Mozambique. So it's probably best not to ask too many questions. Be careful not to be too curious about such things, *mia dolce*, or like The Elephant's Child, you, too, just might encounter a crocodile."

7

That old goosey feeling got me again when I returned to the hotel. It grabbed me as I entered my room with the spare key card and hit the light switch.

Nothing looked out of place, and there was no one in the room but me, so why did I feel uneasy? Why did I feel that someone sinister was there, or had been there? Was it just the knowledge working on me that a stranger had snagged a key to my room? How would they even know what my room number was? The key card wasn't labeled, and the hotel had many rooms.

Had the draperies over the French door been moved? Was the balcony door locked? Were my things as I had left them?

I turned on every light in the room and thought about calling Jay, but he was still out partying. Besides, I knew he would only laugh and call me a ninny.

All seemed to be okay. The room was immaculate. The housekeeper had done her job. There were fresh towels, soap, and tons of toiletries. The bed linens were neatly turned back and a mint and the weather forecast had been placed on the pillow.

Nothing seemed to be wrong or unusual. The stuff in my suitcase looked undisturbed. Nothing seemed to be missing. There was no one in the closet, or the bathroom, or under the bed, and when it all checked out I was glad I hadn't called in the cavalry.

Nevertheless, I couldn't shake the creepy, completely

irrational feeling that someone had been there, pawing through my things and invading my space.

"Go to sleep, Sidney," I told myself as I turned off the bedside lamp, "and try not to be so silly."

H

David warned us all about pickpockets the next morning as we drew near Cape Point and the Cape of Good Hope Nature Reserve.

Jay nudged me. "Heads up, Sidney," he whispered.

"Hush! I can't hear what he is saying because of you."

"These are unusual pickpockets, ladies and gentlemen," David said. "They are easy to spot because they're all wearing fur coats."

"What?" asked Connie. "Did you say fur coats? Who?"

David beamed, glad that someone had taken the bait. He chuckled at his own little joke.

"Yes, indeed I did. Short-haired fur coats. You see, my dears, the Cape area is positively *infested* with Chacma baboons. Baboons! Troops of them. They are known to be purse-snatchers, particularly if there is food in the bag. They have even been known to attack tourists for candy bars in their pockets. So whatever you do here, ladies and gentlemen, do not get off this bus bearing food of any kind. The baboons don't even have to see the food. They have a keen sense of smell, and if they can smell it, they will attack. They are strong and quick and have long, sharp teeth. Not nice or cuddly at all."

"Oh, my," said Wendy, her eyes rounder than ever, "is it safe to even get off the bus?"

"Yes, indeed it is, of course it is, but one must be careful."

Wendy and Tilda put their heads together and spent the rest of the ride into the park planning baboon defense.

The rest of us just enjoyed the scenery as we neared Cape Point, following the paved road as it twisted along the jagged, windswept coastline to the farthest tip of the Cape Peninsula. The land was covered in a hardy scrub called fynbos, an Afrikaans word meaning "fine bush." These fine-leaved, low bushes of the heath are a favorite of the Cape grysbok, and I spotted a grazing antelope, carefully picking its way on long legs among the rocks. It kept a watchful eye, raising its head often as it delicately nibbled the low, tough vegetation. The grays and greens of the rocky, arid landscape formed a dramatic contrast to the vivid blue sky. Now and again I caught a glimpse of a deserted beach far below the roadway on our right.

For the full-day excursion, we were all traveling together in a big bus. The plan was to visit Cape Point and the adjacent Cape of Good Hope Nature Park, then return to Cape Town via Simon's Town. The tour also stopped at a penguin sanctuary called Boulders, and Kirstenboch Gardens on the way back.

Entering the park, we passed lots of animals, including eland, grysbok, Cape mountain zebras, and—surprisingly—ostriches everywhere. I didn't spot any baboons but I wasn't too concerned about them. With Wendy and Tilda on Baboon Patrol, I knew I didn't have to worry about monkeys sneaking up on me.

Rose asked David about the ostriches.

"Oh my, yes," he said. "There are lots of them, dear. They even sell the eggs as souvenirs in the gift shop. The shop has painted ones as well as plain. Some of the painted ones have been made into decorative objects and lamps."

"Gotta have one of those," Jay said, "maybe two."

The bus stopped at the visitor's center.

"This will be quite a long visit, ladies and gentlemen," David said. "We will be here for two hours to give you all time for a good look around. You may visit the lighthouse, have lunch, shop for gifts in the curio shop, and still have plenty of time to take all the pictures you want. Before we begin our visit, however, we want to take a group photo in front of the official Cape of Good Hope sign."

George groaned and said, "Do we have to?"

David looked annoyed, and that feeling was reflected in the frosty tone of his reply. "I will ask that you do, please, everyone, as a personal favor to me and to your host company. It will only take a few moments. Then you may take the funicular up to the old 1860 lighthouse for the splendid view." He looked at his watch. "It's just eleven. We're right on schedule. A lovely lunch, included in your tour, will be served in the Two Oceans Restaurant at twelve. There are tables reserved for us. We'll have an hour for our lunch and shopping and then at one o'clock we will meet back at the bus to leave for Simon's Town. Now if you'll just follow me, we'll pop down that path just over there, take a group photo, and then I'll release you to explore on your own."

Most of us didn't waste any time getting off the bus or heading down the path, though some made a pit stop at the restroom. In a few minutes, we were all being lined up in front of the sign for the group shot.

"Right then, everyone. There," David pointed out, "gather round the sign, please. Now, is everyone here?"

He looked at his list.

"Dennis isn't," said Rose.

"Well, where is he?" asked Mabel, exasperated. "He's always wandering off."

"We'll wait a few minutes more," David said. "He may still be in the loo."

A few moments' delay didn't matter at all, for I could have stood there watching for hours. I was awestruck by the power of the waves at this most southwestern point of Africa. Monster waves constantly crashed onto gigantic granite rocks, sending plumes of sea spray twenty feet into the air.

One powerful wave was followed immediately by another. Thousands of seabirds wheeled overhead, their circling cries muffled by the roar of the churning waves. An occasional fishy whiff from a colony of seals near the base of the cliff mingled with the sea-salt scent on the breeze.

As I stood on the sand, gazing out over the turbulent water, the sea seemed to stretch to infinity. Indeed, there was nothing to be seen beyond the rocks and the breakers but the undulant motion of the gleaming ocean until it met that brilliant blue sky at the horizon.

I couldn't believe I was actually standing at the Cape of Good Hope. I thought back to my seventh-grade geography teacher in my little school back in the red-clay hills of Mississippi, and how she had longed to visit Africa. I wished she could be there with me.

The ferocious power of that water was unbelievable. Seeing its force on such a clear day, in good weather, it was easy to imagine why explorer Bartolomeu Dias named it Cabo Tormentoso, or Cape of Storms, when his ship brought the first Europeans there in 1488. Dias made it around the cape and sailed as far as Kwaaihoek, near the mouth of the Bushman's or Great Fish River, where he erected a large stone cross inscribed with the coat of arms of Portugal. Dias wanted to continue sailing to India, but his crew refused to go any farther, so he was forced to turn his ship around and head back to Portugal.

Almost ten years later, in 1497, Vasco de Gama sailed around the cape and completed the long-hoped-for passage to India. King John was delighted that his men had discovered a way around Africa. He changed the name of the Cape of Storms to the Cape of Good Hope, and so it remains today. Ironically, Dias, on a return voyage in May of 1500, was lost with his ship in a huge storm just off the Cape.

"There he is," David said, spotting Dennis finally coming down the path. "Line up, please, everyone. We're ready now for our photo."

After the group picture was taken, everyone scattered.

Fernando, Jay and I remained, staring at the waves crashing against the giant rocks. Fernando had been there before and told stories of the Cape and the shipwrecks it was famous for causing.

"Many ships have gone down here. This coastline is littered with wrecks."

"Isn't this particular point where the legend of The Flying Dutchman originated?" Jay asked.

"Yes. In 1641 a Dutch ship captain named Van der Decken was battling the fierce storms of the Cape when his ship started sinking. He swore that he would round the Cape if it took until Judgment Day. Sightings of that ghost ship, with its tattered sails and broken masts, have been reported during storms from that time until the present day."

"Creepy," said Jay. "Glad the sun is shining. I sure don't want to see that ship."

"It's eleven-thirty," I said, tearing my eyes away from the boiling sea. "We better get moving if we want to do everything before lunch. We're running late."

"Yeah, thanks to Dennis," Connie said. "That guy is on my last nerve, always wandering off somewhere and making us wait for him. If he keeps it up, I'm going to tell him. I'm going to say my piece."

"I'm going up to the lighthouse," Fernando said. "Would you two like to come with me? That, too, is an amazing view."

I went with him, but Jay declined, saying that he would meet us at lunch. "I need lots of time in the gift shop," he said. "I want to buy an ostrich egg lamp for my apartment. It will take time to choose the perfect one."

⨯

Simon's Town, originally the site of the winter port of the Dutch East India Company, was our next stop. The Dutch had first sailed out of Table Bay, but moved to Simon's Town after they tired of battling the Cape's winter storms. Since 1957, it has been the home port of the South African navy.

We drove through Simon's Town and stopped in the nearby settlement of Boulders, where big granite rocks provide shelter for a colony of over 2,000 African Penguins, formerly called Jackass Penguins. Similar to their South American cousins, they earned that name because of their raucous, braying call.

Jay and I wandered along the boardwalk at Foxy Beach, a part of the Boulders sanctuary. The plank path, built of weathered wood, winds among the giant rocks, allowing visitors an intimate look at the nesting penguins without disturbing the little guys. Because the rocks are so big, the boardwalk offers surprises at every turn. The size of the rocks makes it difficult to see what's coming up next on the path. Beyond the rocks, a beach where people are allowed to swim with the penguins runs into the sea.

"Aren't they cute?" I took the first of dozens of pictures of a nesting pair.

"They are," Jay said, "but don't get too close. If you upset them, they will bite."

"Bite? How can a bird bite? Do they have teeth?"

Jay shrugged. "I don't know, but David said they would. Tell you what, stick your hand down there and see if it's true."

"No, thank you. I'll keep my hands to myself."

Jay stood on the bottom board of the railing, stretching to see past the rocks. He raised his binoculars to his eyes. "Sidney, look. Right there," he leaned toward me, trying to hand me the binoculars, "just past that rock."

"What?" I said, busy with my photography.

"Over there. Dennis. Look at Dennis. What the hell is he doing?"

I focused the binoculars just in time to see Dennis climb over the barrier and disappear among the giant boulders.

"Who knows?" I said. "He had his binoculars with him and David said whales could be seen at this time of year from the beach. Dennis asked a lot of questions about that. Maybe he's going to look for whales."

"Yeah," I said, putting the lens cap back on my camera. "And how typical of him to climb over the barrier to get to the beach instead of taking the normal path, like everyone else! I'm sorry we can't stay longer here, Jay. I'd love to go whale watching, and swim with the penguins. Wouldn't that be fun?"

Arms akimbo, Jay replied, "No, Sidney, it would not. David said there are great white sharks off this beach, babe. Want to swim with them? You can even buy a cage dive, right in the middle of them. Hey, that gives me a great idea. If Dennis wants a cage dive, we can hold the bus and I'll pay. Bet I could take up a collection without any trouble. Maybe Mabel would like to go, too."

We started walking down the boardwalk back towards the visitor's center. I saw something tiny and cuddly in a little hole near a rock.

"Look, Jay," I said, grabbing his arm, "down there in the rocks. See that little baby? Down there, in the nest, just a fluff of gray feathers. He's cute, isn't he? They're all so cute. Strange, but cute. Such odd little birds."

Jay's attention was elsewhere. "Well, the penguins are odd birds, for sure, but the oddest bird of all just climbed back over the fence. Here he comes. He's headed back toward the bus. Maybe that means he won't keep us all waiting this time."

"Well, he better not keep us waiting again today, or Connie's going to be on him like white on rice."

Jay laughed at that as we left the boardwalk, "Come on, Scarlett, let's go. You've got enough penguin shots. I want to check out the penguin gift shop. I might find something else to add to my collection."

8

"This is just a little ol' bitty baby airport," said Connie the following afternoon, as our small plane landed and we taxied into Hoedspruit.

She was right. The terminal was tiny, a group of small buildings, some of them open-air. It was not anything like the kind of normal, security-strict giant airport that we all knew so well.

We deplaned, passed by the souvenir shops, identified our bags for the safari lodge staff, and headed for the exit.

The driveway outside the toy terminal was crowded with safari jeeps, vans, and trucks. David and a representative from our game lodge directed us to a group of Land Rovers parked under the thin shade of a thorn tree.

"Oh my goodness, look at those enormous safari cars, Tilda! Isn't this exciting!"

"Heavens, yes, Wendy! It's quite wonderful, isn't it?"

"Group up, group up, keep moving, walk, walk, walk," George said in a low voice, and Rich, Chris, Fernando, Connie, Jay, and I moved quickly through the crowd to the line of waiting Land Rovers.

These were not your typical soccer-mom-with-a-lot-of-cash Land Rovers. These vehicles were big, hulking, and rugged. They were built to take a lot of abuse over rough terrain and resembled army vehicles. I wondered if they were also built to withstand animal attacks. I didn't want to find out.

Burly drivers with the Leopard Dance Lodge logo on

their shirts took our hand luggage before helping us climb up into the dark green, open-air Land Rovers.

The lodge logo was a snarling leopard lying on the branch of a stylized tree that formed the words "Leopard Dance." It was painted on the doors of all the lodge's vehicles. Our luggage was loaded into a big open truck and covered with a tarp.

Yet again, everyone had to wait on Dennis, who finally emerged from the men's room. He was trying unsuccessfully to yuck it up with a clearly annoyed driver who had been sent to find him. What was with this guy?

Dennis climbed into the Land Rover behind us, taking the only empty seat, which happened to be next to dreadful old Mabel. She jammed her safari hat down on her stick-straight red hair and pulled the cord tight under her chin. She began spraying insect repellent on her bony arms while staring with disdain at the peddlers who milled about the parked vehicles, hawking their wares. Mabel glared at the brightly clad women and children as if she would like to spray them, too.

"I think Dennis has found a buddy," said Connie.

"Yeah," George said. "What a pair! Wouldn't you just love to spray them both? Maybe some magic spray, so we could make them both disappear."

Jay, seated next to me on the back row of the three-row, open-top vehicle, whispered in my ear. "I don't know if you've noticed, Sidney, but our drivers are not exactly smiling staffers. They look pretty tough, like prison guards at Rikers."

He was right. The men from the other lodges were all smiling, laughing, joking, and just generally chatting up their new guests and each other. Ours were all very muscular and mostly silent, speaking only when necessary, looking grim and all business. I felt a sudden chill, despite the heat. Who knew what this adventure would bring? It was supposedly perfectly safe, but then so is a cruise, and it would be hard to imagine a situation more dangerous than my last one. Not for the first time, I wondered whether danger was following me— if I was under some kind of big jinx. Maybe a voodoo spell. After all, this was Africa. What a bad thought that was. I forced my mind away from it, trying to rekindle the excitement of the safari.

The lead jeep, with Wendy and Tilda bending David's ear in the front seat, pulled away from the parking area and drove through the gate onto the main road.

Our driver, a giant black man named Vincent, followed. Vincent carried a heavy, deadly-looking rifle in a special holster mounted on the jeep at his right side, available at a moment's notice. The steel of the barrel was as blue-black and smooth as his skin and the similarity between man and gun did not end there. Both were powerful, silent and efficient. Vincent was a giant of a man, with broad shoulders straining the fabric of his safari tan shirt and a wide, flat face with small, alert eyes. Those eyes missed little. Even behind the dark aviator glasses, those eyes were always watching. A bill cap embroidered with the Leopard Dance logo was jammed down tight over close-cropped dark hair. He wore a knife on his belt, and I imagined that there might be a handgun hidden somewhere close by. Vincent was clearly accustomed to danger and seemed fully capable of handling it.

An equally imposing and muscular armed man named Anthony rode in the game spotter's seat, which is mounted on the front left fender of the vehicle. Like Vincent, Anthony had a perennially wary air about him. He clearly didn't miss much, either, but his rounder face and chubby belly made him seem somewhat more accessible. He was dressed like Vincent, armed with a long knife in a scabbard on his belt, and he had a pair of powerful binoculars hanging from his burly neck. Before clambering into his seat he had stowed a machete next to Vincent. Neither was a man you would willingly antagonize.

Each safari vehicle has one driver and one game spotter. I was told that the driver does not usually change, but the spotter sometimes does.

The other vehicles from our game lodge were behind us, with the luggage truck bringing up the rear, stirring up a thick cloud of dust. The drivers were careful not to follow too close. It was almost October—the end of winter and the beginning of the South African spring. Though the nights were cold, the days were delightful. That was a special treat for us, for in New York, winter was fast approaching. It was extremely dry, too. The rains had not yet begun.

Near the airport the land along the main paved road was fenced for the most part. Then, as we sped along the tarmac, the chain-link ended and the road was bordered instead with a dense scrub, thorn thickets, and leafless trees. The landscape was stark and dramatic. It was not a very pretty time of year, but great for a safari because the animals are easier to spot in the early spring before the leaves emerge on the vegetation to hide them.

Before long we turned off the paved road and bumped over a shallow ditch to the left, onto a dry, dirt track. The vehicles spread out even farther because of the increased dust.

Vincent was driving slowly, silently communicating with Anthony through looks and nods. Anthony's head moved constantly from left to right, scanning the bush. In just a few minutes, the lead jeep was no longer in sight. When I turned to look behind us, the other vehicles seemed to have vanished as well.

We lurched across a shallow ditch, wheels spinning in the dry, sandy soil of the empty creek-bed. Then we turned left again, going deeper into the scrub, bumping over rocks. Branches scraped the sides of the vehicle. I grabbed at the side of the Rover, trying to brace myself.

"Please keep your hands inside the vehicle and mind your heads," Vincent warned.

Everyone was chattering away, heads swiveling, watching for animals. Small wooden signposts at a crossroads in the track pointed the way to our lodge and also to other game camps. Because of the bumpy trail, Vincent drove at a crawl, pausing occasionally, sometimes almost stopping. Then, apparently in response to some silent signal from Anthony, he turned off the engine and we rolled to a stop.

Everyone abruptly stopped talking and the only sound you could hear was the ticking of the cooling engine and the lone cry of a bird.

"Just there," Anthony said in a low voice, pointing to our right, "giraffe."

"Oh, my goodness, y'all, look at that," Connie whispered.

We sat staring, camera shutters clicking, as a pair of giraffes moved gracefully through the bush, pausing now and then to pluck leaves with their long, blue-black tongues from the tops of the acacia trees. Finally, majestically, they moved on, striding smoothly out of sight.

"Welcome to Africa," Vincent said as he started the engine. He turned right at another crossroads, drove about a mile along a smaller track bordered by tall dry grass, and then passed under a large rustic sign carved with the snarling leopard logo. The heavy sign was supported by massive carved poles planted on either side of the road.

There appeared to be no gates, no fences. We were in a private game reserve, one of many clustered along the edges of Kruger National Park. Apparently the owners and staff of each lodge just knew where their property ended and another's began, for no boundaries were apparent. To the visitor, except for the gateposts, it was impossible to tell. It all looked the same.

In our safari orientation David had explained to us that the western boundary of the Kruger National Park is lined by a crazy quilt of private reserves, most featuring lavish lodges, luxury tented camps or exclusive bush camps. He had shown

MARIE MOORE

pictures of some of the camps that were represented by his company.

He told us that a park boundary fence, built in the 1960s between Kruger and the private reserves, blocked the natural migration routes of the animals for many years. Later, by mutual agreement, the fence was removed and the animals now moved freely back and forth across the land. They could even wander at will throughout our camp.

Driving faster now, headed to the lodge, Vincent pointed to the big thatched roof of a large house off to our right, just visible through the brush.

"Big boss house. The owner of Leopard Dance, Mr. van der Brugge."

"That is one fabulous house," Chase said. "It's amazing. Check out that airstrip behind it! Will we meet Mr. van der Brugge?"

"Not today," Vincent said.

"Tomorrow, then?"

"Maybe. Maybe not. He is a busy man. I do not know."

We pulled up to the main lodge entrance, where the lead car with David and the others had stopped and was now unloading.

Just past the big boss's grand house, the dusty one-lane track widened enough to allow two vehicles to pass. The thorny scrub gave way to a small meadow of tall brown grass. On the other side of it, men in Leopard Dance safari clothes and women in bright woven cotton skirts and headdresses lined up to welcome us on the steps of a tall, open-air pavilion.

The buildings were sturdy, built with thick, mud-colored walls, and roofed with strong, hand-hewn beams supporting heavy silver thatch. The whole camp was stark yet impressive and fit well into the surrounding bush.

Climbing down from the vehicles, we were offered welcome drinks. A slender, smiling girl in native dress invited us to sit and relax in the open-air pavilion while we checked in and awaited the arrival of the entire group.

"This is great," Rich said, sipping his drink and leaning back in a leather chair. He was watching an African Hornbill preen itself on the branch of a nearby tree, "Just as I pictured it. Fantastic."

"*Karibu*, ladies and gentlemen, *karibu*! That is Swahili for welcome! May I have your attention, please?"

A tiny woman stood in the center of the room, also wearing a floor-length native dress of bright printed cotton. Her hair was wrapped in a turban of matching fabric, and bracelets encircled her slim brown arms. She stood, smiling, by the circular stone fire-pit, clapping her delicate little hands.

"Welcome to Leopard Dance, my friends. Welcome! We are happy that you have come to be our guests. My name is Rebecca, and if there is anything at all that you need while you are here, you must tell me right away. Life here is very simple, and very relaxing, you will see. Please listen now as I mention our little routines that we hope you will all enjoy."

She handed each of us a printed brochure, which listed a schedule and descriptions of the safari camp's facilities.

"Soon you will be shown to your rooms," she continued, "and you may relax as you wish until the bell rings for the evening game drive. Each day we have two game drives, one in the morning, and one in the evening. This evening, the game drive will depart from this pavilion at six o'clock. When you return, drinks and dinner will be served in the main dining pavilion at approximately eight o'clock."

"Do we have to go on the game drive?" Chase asked. "Or can we just stay in the camp?"

Rich groaned.

"You may do as you wish," said Rebecca, smiling. "It is your vacation."

Chase smirked back at Rich and ordered another drink.

"In the morning," Rebecca continued, "and each

morning while you are here, you will be awakened by a tap on your door at first light. A guard will be there with your preference of tea or coffee. When you are ready, he will escort you back to this place to depart for the morning game drive. Please dress warmly. At this time of year it is still very cold in the mornings, but we will have blankets for you in the safari vehicles."

Tilda and Wendy started whispering to each other, no doubt over what they would wear to keep warm. They took great pains to be properly outfitted at all times for any weather.

Mabel shushed them as Rebecca continued her speech. "After viewing the animals, you will be returned to camp for hot drinks and breakfast. During the day it will be warm. You may relax by the pool, visit our spa, and have lunch. In the late afternoon, we will have another game drive, then cocktails, followed by dinner. This is our routine."

Rebecca paused. She looked at each of us in turn, her smile gone, her voice suddenly serious. "We have very few rules here at Leopard Dance, my friends. Life is simple and relaxing. But we do have certain rules which must be followed. Please pay close attention."

As she spoke, she ticked off the rules with her delicate fingers. "One, there are areas that are not open at all to guests and these are clearly marked, as you will see. Please do not enter these restricted areas. Two, please do not approach any animals. As you have been told and may have observed, the camp is not fenced. The animals wander in and out as they wish. Remember that while these animals are beautiful, they are also wild. We do not want anyone to be hurt. Wild animals can be dangerous. Then there is the third rule, the most important of all, which cannot ever be broken. It must be strictly observed by everyone."

Now she had the entire group's full attention. Even Tilda and Wendy were still, staring at Rebecca with their round blue eyes.

"At night, no one—no one at all—may stroll around the camp without escort for any reason. Our guards are fully armed, and they will come to your doors to take you to dinner and back or wherever else you need to go in the camp. You have only to call them and wait. There will be no wandering about alone. This is the most important rule that you must all obey, for your own safety, without exception. I hope that everyone understands this rule."

She smiled again then, and looked at each one of us in turn. Then, apparently satisfied, she nodded, and clapped her little hands. Another beautiful girl, in similar dress, appeared with a tray of large brass keys.

"That is enough serious talk. Here is Winsome, with your room keys. When you have collected your things and have finished your drinks, you will be shown to your rooms just over there."

She pointed to a dusty path leading from the welcome pavilion through the tall grass and thorn trees to a series of thatched huts.

"The spa is the first large building on your right. You can make appointments there for treatments and massages. The dining room is in the largest building at the far end of the camp. Just follow the path. That is also where the swimming pool is located, along with the bar and the library. There is no television. There are no computers, no telephones. You are completely isolated from the world. We want you to forget about all the cares of civilization for a little while. Just be one with nature. Enjoy the animals, listen to the birds, and relax with us. Welcome to Africa!"

She bowed and everyone clapped.

"Now Winsome will distribute your keys," she concluded, smiling once more, "and your escorts will take you to your rooms. Mr. Wilson, Miss Marsh, you will be sharing Hut No. 1. Please follow Felix. Your luggage has already been delivered." She continued down the list, assigning huts to our fellow group members.

When she finished, everyone moved to collect the hand luggage. Jay and I followed yet another beefy giant in a tan, safari lodge uniform down a winding dusty path toward a small mud-covered, thatched hut on the bank of a narrow, dry riverbed.

"This seems pretty grim, Sidney," Jay whispered as we followed Felix down the dusty path through the scrub. "Not exactly what I was expecting. I think we're screwed. I mean, the pavilion was nice enough, and the drinks were good, but that hut up ahead there is the pits. Just look at it. It's authentic, all right. I think that's real dung on the walls. And I thought we would at least have our own rooms."

"Hush. He'll hear you. Silverstein signed us up together. It's not the first time we've shared a room. Get with the program, Jay. Where is your spirit of adventure? This is the African bush. What were you expecting, Vegas?"

Jay made a silent but meaningful gesture that Felix did not see. A little over halfway down, the path branched, with the right fork leading to Hut No. 1 and the left leading to Hut No. 2. Small, rustic signposts pointed the way.

Felix unlocked the door of hut No. 1 for us, then headed quietly back up the path toward the pavilion, vanishing from sight among the thorn bushes.

9

Hut No. 1 was fabulous.

Jay and I were both stunned. The round, thatched, mud-daub building sure hadn't looked like much from the dirt path outside. Its simplicity had deceived us.

"Nice," Jay said, taking it all in. "I was so wrong. This is really, really nice."

A pair of queen-size, hand-carved wooden four-poster beds with luxurious linens, each draped in gauzy white mosquito netting, dominated the spacious room. The beds faced a sliding glass wall that opened onto a small deck overlooking the river.

Heavy, wooden floor-to-ceiling louvered panels were fitted into a track to slide closed over the glass wall as needed. The wooden panels were also equipped with locks so that the glass wall could be safely left open with the shutters closed. That feature allowed the wind and the sounds of the birds and animals to flow in through the louvers.

Ceiling fans turned lazily, stirring the fragrance of flowers that had been placed in low vases all around the room. The floors were of gleaming dark wood accented with bright, handwoven rugs.

The big bathroom also had sliding glass walls on the river side, a stone floor, and an enormous Jacuzzi tub. There were stacks of thick towels, jars of designer bath salts, soaps and lotions, and terrycloth robes. A separate glass shower had its own dressing room, which opened on an outdoor shower enclosed by a tall bamboo fence.

"This bathroom might be bigger than your apartment in New York, Sidney. And check this out, babe, even the throne-room can be open-air."

He slid the shutters and glass wall aside to expose the toilet to the open air.

"Thanks, but no thanks, Jay. I'll be keeping that door closed and locked for sure."

Back in the main room, on the left side of the entryway, a cooler in the wet bar held crystal wine glasses and bottles of South African wine. Near it was a woven basket of cheese, crackers, and fruit.

Jay grabbed a bottle and a corkscrew, while I peered into drawers and cupboards. Our bags had been unpacked and our clothes put away in massive wardrobes of carved wood. The primitive yet intricate carvings depicted abstract animals, trees, and birds. We admired the matching carvings on the four posts, headboards and footboards of the beds.

"Don't even start," I said to Jay, reading his mind. "You could never get any of it home to your apartment. Too big, too heavy."

"Yeah, I know it," he sighed, "but it would be really fabulous, wouldn't it?"

The sliding glass walls on the river side opened to a small deck with lounge chairs and a hammock.

"Now THIS is more like it!" Jay said, pouring us each a glass of wine. "I like this. I like this a lot. This is more my style."

He opened the sliding glass wall and stepped out onto the little deck overlooking the edge of the riverbed.

"Oh, poop. Sidney, look at this. Looks like Hut No. 1 had visitors last night."

I joined him on the deck and followed his gaze to a pair of uprooted saplings, some broken branches, a tree with stripped bark and lots of enormous brown balls of elephant dung, obviously fresh. Jay took a photo.

"This dry riverbed looks like a main path for a lot of animals," I said. As if to prove my point, a big, male eland appeared around the bend. He stopped when he saw us, head up, sniffing the wind. After deciding we were harmless, he continued on past, breaking into a run when he was just below our deck. Neither Jay nor I was quick enough to catch it on camera, though, so stunned were we by its appearance.

After it passed, I noticed that the sandy riverbed was covered with spoor—poop and tracks of wild animals—and a few human footprints.

We heard a tap just then at the main door. When I opened it, the small, lovely key-woman entered, bringing flashlights and a battery-powered lantern.

"Hello," she said. "I am Winsome, remember me? I am the night maid. Welcome to Leopard Dance. These lights are for your use if you should need them. Here in the bush, the power often fails. There are also lots of candles and matches just here, in this cupboard. But you must be very, very careful if you light candles. Never leave candles burning when you are not in the room or when you are sleeping, yes? Fire is a great danger for all of us. We are all afraid of fire." She gestured toward the thatched roof, as if to emphasize her point.

After placing the lantern on the shelf, she pointed to a cord just to the right of the door. "Ring this bell—this one, here by the door—if you need anything or to summon the guard. We want you to be very, very comfortable here. If there is anything at all that you need or want, you have only to ask. Is there anything else that I can bring you before I say good evening?"

We had no requests or questions, so we thanked her and she smiled and bowed her way out as I closed and locked the door.

"Want the first shower?" Jay called from the bathroom, though clearly he really did. He was already unbuttoning his shirt.

"No, thanks, it's okay, you go first. I'm fine."

I knew that he needed more time than I did to get dressed. Jay had been planning his safari ensemble for days and he needed ample time to fine-tune it. I just wanted a quick bath and a fresh change of clothes.

I refilled my glass and stretched out in the hammock on the back deck to wait my turn. Just as I settled in, I heard a branch break and turned toward the sound in time to see Dennis walking steadily along the dry riverbed below, headed away from the camp.

Now where could he be going? I thought. The shadows were lengthening, sunset was not far away. But he didn't see me folded in my hammock, and I sure didn't call out to him. In another minute he was around the bend and out of sight.

"Sidney, it's your turn," Jay called.

I stepped back into the room and got my first glimpse of Jay in full *African Queen* garb. He clearly thought he was channeling Bogart, or maybe Bacall. He kept turning in front of the mirror, admiring himself, making minor adjustments here and there.

He was clad entirely in khaki, wearing canvas pants and a shirt with a lot of pockets topped by a photo vest. Expensive leather boots and a safari hat pinned up on one side with a feather completed the ensemble. A tooth or claw or something hung from a leather cord around his neck inside his half-open shirt. The only thing missing was a knife at his belt, but I guess maybe he couldn't bring that on the plane.

"Drum roll, please," he said, striking a pose. "Well, what do you think? Looking good? Looking great?"

"Looking great, Jay. Really great. Is that your molar hanging around your neck?"

He didn't bother to answer that, just grabbed his camera and binoculars and marched out, saying, "I'm going to check out the spa. Come when the bell rings, smartass, or you'll be left."

H

I stayed way too long in that amazingly deep bathtub, so I barely had time to pull on some jeans, a T-shirt, and a pullover when the bell rang. Not wanting to be left, I ran down the path to the jeeps.

Jay, still in a huff over my lack of appreciation for his outfit, had not saved me a seat, but bless his heart, George had. I climbed into the Land Rover, and in a few moments, we were off on our first game drive.

10

The dark-green Land Rovers rolled out from the safari lodge in single file, each with a driver/guide and a game spotter riding on a seat mounted on the front fender. The two men worked as an efficient team, communicating almost silently to follow or find animals. It is amazing, really, the animals that an experienced spotter can see in the deep camouflage of the bush.

Some of the group, including Chase, had chosen to stay behind at the pool and the bar. I couldn't imagine that. I mean, why even come? I didn't want to miss one single moment of a game drive.

As the great orange ball of sun began to sink, the temperature dipped as well, and we huddled beneath green wool blankets. The cold air rushed through the open vehicles as we sped along the road, making conversation difficult, if not impossible.

Jay had taken the seat behind the driver, next to Rich. I was in the next row with George, and Connie and Fernando were behind us. The lead jeep, just in front of us, held David, Wendy and Tilda Smithwick, Rose Abrams, and Mabel whatever from Iowa. I still didn't know her last name. I only knew that she was trouble and should be avoided whenever possible.

Mabel could have been the model for a cartoon drawing of an old maid schoolteacher, with her stringy reddish-brown straight hair, little squinty eyes behind sixties-era wire-rims, a long thin nose, thin lips, and a permanently righteous expression. Pinched-up. That's what they would call her back home. She had been assigned to room with Rose Abrams for the trip, and it was clear that the pairing was not a success. Rose, a short, plump, pleasant woman with dark curly hair and a warm smile, sat as far from Mabel as she could on the leather seat.

The last vehicle held five strangers, all of whom I had not yet met, and Irene, Connie's roommate, who was French or maybe North African, and very chic. She was not a travel agent and was at the lodge on vacation from her job with some international company. I didn't know if the others were late-arriving travel agents or regular paying guests of the lodge like Irene.

The safari vehicles began to spread out from one another. The one in front of us turned off to the right, down a grassy track, while we continued on the main track.

I realized then that I had not seen Dennis, who was George's roommate, in any of the vehicles.

"Where's Dennis?" I shouted.

"I don't know," George yelled back. "I didn't stay any longer than I had to in the room. When I left he was lying on his bed, reading a newspaper. The front page had banner headlines identifying that dead guy they found in the hotel garden."

I had to wait a few minutes until we slowed down a bit to ask more. Finally I could speak without shouting. "Who was it?"

"Who?"

"The dead guy."

"Oh, I forgot the name. No one you'd know. He had a criminal record, was mixed up in a lot of bad stuff, smuggling, drugs, I don't know. Bad stuff."

"Did he die of natural causes or was he killed?"

"Killed. Stabbed. But no arrest has been made. If they have any suspects, they're not releasing that information. The story said the investigation is ongoing."

My thoughts went back to that night, not for the first time. In my mind's eye, I smelled the fragrant flowers, heard again the rustle of the wind through the trees. Had I heard anything else, anyone else? Who were those men I had seen?

I remembered then, with a start, that the man I had met at Table Mountain had not contacted me before we left Cape Town. I wondered if he would. Or if he could. The front desk at our Waterfront hotel knew our destination and the contact information. Did they ever give that information out? We would be returning to the same hotel after the safari. Maybe I would hear from him then. Unless he was somehow involved in the murder and being questioned.

"George, I'd like to see that article Where did Dennis get the newspaper?"

"I don't know. He was reading it when I came into the room. It might still be there."

"Why didn't Dennis come with us on the game drive? Was he afraid, like Chase?"

"I don't think so. He said he was coming when he returned to the hut with the newspaper. But then he changed his mind, said he wasn't feeling well. He had a headache and was going to skip the evening game drive and grab a nap. He hoped to sleep until dinner."

That's odd, I thought. He wasn't sleeping when I last saw him. He was marching down the riverbed as if he was in a hurry.

"Look, y'all, oh, look!" Connie shrieked, "There's an elephant."

Vincent, the driver, motioned for silence, turned off the engine, and rolled to a stop in the middle of the dirt road. It was blocked by a clearly unhappy bull elephant that stood about seventy-five feet in front of us, silhouetted against the setting sun, flapping his ears.

"He is angry," Vincent said in a low voice. "He thinks the

road is his. We will wait. We will watch. Be very quiet."

The elephant spread his ears wide, held his head high, and made a false charge toward us. Then he stopped, shaking those big ears.

"As far as I'm concerned, he can have this road," George said in a nervous whisper. "The road *is* his. It's his road. He was here first. Back up, Vincent, and let him have it."

Vincent motioned for George to be still. "He will not harm us unless we challenge him. He knows our vehicles. As long as we respect him, there is no problem. He knows we are not hunters. There is little the elephant fears except hunters."

"Well, what about lions?" Connie asked. "Isn't he afraid of lions?"

"No. Because they are so big, the adult elephant has no enemies other than people. Lions only attack young calves, or the sick or lame. Never a healthy adult like this one. He is not afraid of the lion. The lion fears him."

After what seemed like forever—but was in actuality probably only five minutes or so—the big beast lost interest in us. He left the road, flapping those big ears and heading off to the right into the bush. Only the setting sun, firing the horizon as it turned the sky orange and rose and crimson, was visible at the end of the road.

Everyone started talking at once, excited about the elephant, excited about the pictures they had taken. The thrill of actually seeing an elephant so near—not confined in a cage or an enclosure but moving freely about—was unforgettable.

Vincent started the engine and gunned it down the path. "We must hurry now. The sun is setting. We are late."

Jay turned around in his seat, apparently no longer mad at me for not appreciating his wardrobe.

"I'll bet he has to get us all out of the reserve before dark and that's just fine. I like that. Dumbo's daddy scared the hell out of me."

Just as Jay spoke, Vincent made a sharp right off the road and into the bush.

"Not home," George said. "Detour."

We lurched over a rock and up onto a faint trek. Thorn bushes scraped the sides of the vehicle.

"Hold on," Vincent said. "Watch your arms. Keep them inside."

Just ahead in the gathering dusk, we saw the other Rovers parked. Their passengers milled around a folding table that had been set up as a bar.

"Nice," Fernando said behind me. "Sundowners."

"What are Sundowners?" I asked.

"Drinks. Wine, cocktails, served *al fresco* in the South African bush. A lovely tradition."

"You have got to be kidding," Jay said, twisting around in his seat. "They want us to get out of the car, when it's getting dark, with a bunch of wild animals all around? That's nuts. Risk my life for a little glass of cheap wine? No way."

The others climbed down, joined the rest of the group, and ordered drinks. Jay didn't move and neither did I.

"Jay. It's okay. They wouldn't do this if it weren't safe."

"Sidney, I'm trying really hard to be a good sport about all this but when I signed on for the trip, nobody said anything about walking around at night in the open in a game park. That elephant was bad enough, but at least I was in a car that could drive away. Now they want me to get out of the car and stroll around like a target. That can't be safe. That's not my idea of fun. And you know how I feel about wild animals. I think they're beautiful. I have photographs of them and I use animal print fabric in my apartment. But I don't like close contact. You know that. Not happening, Sidney. No way."

"I know. It's fine. Do what you want. Don't worry about it. If you don't feel comfortable, just stay in the Rover, but I'm going ahead with the others. Here, keep my binoculars. You might spot something while we're gone."

I gave him a pat, climbed down, and started for the party, feeling sorry for him. I hated that he was missing such a unique and fabulous experience because of his fears.

I am a country girl, from a little town in the Deep South. I played outside all the time as a child, learning the ways of the woods. My grandfather had a farm, and many of my relatives were hunters and fishermen. We all rode horses at an early age, and everyone had lots of dogs and cats. I grew up interacting with animals, only mine were not so exotic. I respect wild animals. I realize what they can do, but I am not petrified of them the way Jay is.

Like Chase and George, Jay is a city boy. He comes from a small industrial town in Pennsylvania. His hometown had parks instead of woods, and he moved to New York as soon as he got a chance. I thought the urban upbringing had a lot to do with the fear these three men shared. Nature was just out of the realm of their experience.

Jay sat in the Rover for a while by himself before finally giving up and joining us. Maybe boredom conquered his fear, or maybe he got scared being alone in the Rover in the dark. For whatever reason, I was surprised but glad to see him at the table ordering a drink.

"Vincent, where is the bathroom?" Connie asked, after we had all been served. "I gotta go."

"There is no bathroom, lady. You must go there, in the tall grass, out of the circle of light. Take a friend with you. One of you go. One of you keep watch."

"Keep watch for what?"

Vincent just looked at her.

"Keep watch for the lions, that's what," Jay said, moving closer to Vincent and his rifle. "The hungry ones. The lions who are hunting for their dinner. Can't you wait, Connie? I'm not going. Not even if I have to pee in my pants. Do you really, really have to go?"

Connie made a face at him. "Yes, I do," she said. "I totally can't wait."

"I'll walk with you, Connie," I said, setting my empty

glass on the table. "I might as well go, too."

"Scream if something comes," George said. "So we can run for the jeeps."

They would, I thought, *and they'd drive away, too.*

Tending to your business in the near-dark African bush is a tense experience, to say the least. We didn't linger, and were mighty glad to step back into the clearing.

"How was it?" George called out, as we joined the group.

"Scary," Connie said, "and that sage grass tickled."

"Be glad that's all that tickled."

When cocktail time ended, we climbed back into the vehicles to head back to camp for the evening meal. Anthony, the giant game spotter riding in the seat on the front fender, turned on a big spotlight that he played on the branches above us as we went. Vincent drove slowly now in the gathering darkness.

"Anthony looks for leopard," Vincent said.

Jay shuddered. He was scanning the tree limbs with his binoculars more intently than Anthony.

"How much fun is this?" I said to him, trying to get his mind off leopards. "Don't you think it's exciting?"

I was apparently fully back in favor. He had taken the seat next to me for the ride home.

Ignoring my remark, he stared grimly through his binoculars as we rushed through the now pitch-black night.

"What are you looking for, Jay? It's totally dark. You can't possibly see anything."

"Eyes. You can see eyes in the dark."

"Oh. Okay." I tried again. "Didn't you just love the sundowners?"

"No, Sidney, I did not. I did not like it at all. What is there to like about standing defenseless out in the open, in the dark, having drinks with wild animals all around? They were probably circling, watching us, smelling us, trying to decide which one of us would taste best. What is so great about that?

What is to keep a lion from just sneaking up and biting my ass? I ask you, what?"

He was on his podium now, center stage, really winding up. "In Kenya they won't allow you to ride in open vehicles, Sidney, and you absolutely are not allowed to even step out of the car, much less get out and walk around. Here, they have you riding in a convertible, and they set up a table in the open and have cocktails. I ask you, why would it *not* be safe in Kenya but it *is* safe here? Are the Kenyan lions hungrier than these lions? I don't think so."

"The tourist rules are just different here, Jay," Fernando said.

"Oh, okay, okay. That explains it. Do the lions know the rules?"

"Well," I said, "what about the Masai tribe in Kenya, Jay? They just walk around everywhere, out in the open, all over the Masai Mara, and the lions don't eat them. What about that?"

Connie chimed in. "Well, see, I think the lions ate some of them one time and didn't like the way they tasted. The Masai wear those red robes all the time and so the lions have learned that the red ones have a funny taste that they don't like so they just leave them alone. Kind of like a little kid knows that the broccoli he hates the taste of is green, you know what I mean?"

Jay hooted. "No, Connie, no one ever knows what you mean and neither do you. All I know is, this little soiree in the dark is no fun. It makes me nervous. I don't like it. I don't think clients would like it, either, especially High Steppers."

"I think it is romantic, this tiny brush with danger," Fernando said. "I will look forward to tomorrow's sundowners."

"Do they do this every night?" George asked.

"Not every night," Jay groaned.

"Every night," said Vincent, as he turned onto the main lodge road toward home.

11

It was the leopard track that really did it for Jay.

Back in camp after our first game drive, we had stopped by our hut to leave our cameras and freshen up. And after a glass or four of that excellent South African wine and another costume change in our comfortable lodging, Jay's fears had subsided a bit. By dinnertime, he had mellowed out and was pretty much back to normal. Well, normal for him.

Felix knocked on our door to escort us to dinner. He was holding a big green lantern and an even bigger rifle.

"Whoa, there," Jay said. "That's quite a cannon you've got there, Felix. Do you know how to use that, big guy?"

Felix just grinned and nodded.

"Good," Jay said.

The evening was crisp and clear, with a slight breeze. We followed Felix and his powerful light down the dusty path through the brush.

Our hut, No. 1, was closest to the camp entrance, and thus farther than any of the others from the dining lodge. After collecting us, Felix made a couple of stops to pick up others.

"Wait here for me in the main path while I bring these ladies," he said. "It will only take a moment. Keep your flashlights on and do not go on ahead without me."

"Don't you worry about that, my friend," Jay said, peering into the gloom. "We're not moving without you. And tell those ladies to hurry their asses up."

Jay was on his third 360, scanning the bushes, shining his

flashlight like a beacon, when he saw it on the path just ahead.

A fresh leopard track. A big one.

And, just ahead of it, another, and another.

"Dear God," he said. "That baby really is around here somewhere. FELIX!"

Felix came running, with Connie and Irene right behind him. He looked at the tracks, motioning for us to be still. Then he spoke quietly in what I think was Bantu into his radio. David had said that the local dialect was Bantu, though some spoke Xhosa and most also spoke Swahili. In seconds, two burly guards joined us on the path, shining their lights on the tracks.

"He has made a kill," one of them said, pointing to dark drops in the sand. You could see where something heavy had been dragged along the edge of the path.

"Do not worry," Felix said to us. "He will not be back. He will take his prize home to the limb of a tree. He will not hunt again until he has eaten and slept and is hungry once more."

"Well, that's okay, then, isn't it? Perfect, just perfect," said Jay. "Isn't that just great? That particular leopard is not stalking us any more tonight because he has already grabbed his dinner. Woo-hoo, I'm so relieved! Now aren't we having fun, out here in the dark with no fence around us, right smack in the middle of Africa? Move it, ladies, just get moving. Let's get inside that dining hall quick, just in case that big guy has a buddy around here somewhere who hasn't had his snack yet."

♓

Our first dinner exceeded all our expectations, with several courses of wild game, fish, fresh vegetables, cheese, and delightful desserts, all accompanied by way too much of that delicious wine. We all applauded as Chef Willem was introduced along with his staff. Chef Willem, David said, had immigrated to South Africa from neighboring Zimbabwe.

"I understand that he had a rough go of it," David said, "like so many others. Dreadful situation. Simply dreadful! He is a fine cook, though, I must say. *Ripping* good fortune for the camp to have got him. His cuisine is *divine!*"

I had to agree. The food really was delicious.

Even after—or maybe because of—the excitement on the path, everyone was full of conversation. The satisfying dinner and shared experiences helped create a mellow mood both during and after our meal.

We sat in deep leather chairs after dinner in front of the fire circle. Sipping coffee and the last of the wine, we laughed, told tales, and watched animals come to drink from the water hole. We swapped war stories, funny things that had happened in our jobs, but Jay really made them laugh when he explained why he thought we had been allowed to go on safari even after the fiasco of our last cruise.

"Sidney and I ran into a little trouble on our last trip out, see, so it was hard to understand why our boss, Mr. Silverstein, rewarded us with this luxury fam. Silverstein is not known for his generosity. Now, after seeing that leopard track, I know why. He wants to see if it's safe before he sends his good clients here. If we make it back safe and sound, okay, fine, he can sell the trip. If we don't make it back, well, that's okay, too. We are the sacrifice."

No one missed electronic entertainment at all. It was comfortable, telling stories and jokes before a fire with friends. Everyone seemed reluctant for the pleasant evening to end.

The lodge was open on one side, facing an infinity swimming pool. On the far end of the pool was the almost-dry river bed, which widened at that point to form a large watering hole.

Although the river held little water before the rains, a small amount remained in the muddy pool. Three wart hogs appeared at the far edge for a drink.

"Look at them," said Connie. "Aren't they cute? Look at

their little tails twirling! I mean, they are so ugly they are cute."

"They remind me of Dennis," Jay said. "Something about the face. Do you think Dennis is so ugly he's cute, Connie?"

"Now is that nice?" I said.

"No, but neither is Dennis," George said.

"Actually," said Connie, "they remind me of my second husband."

"How many husbands have you had?" asked Rose.

"Three. The last one died six months ago. I'm looking for another."

"Got anyone in mind?" said Fernando.

"No, darlin', but I'm looking for a real old guy this time. A fella with a lot of money, no children, and a bad heart. If you see an old boy like that, you let me know."

Fernando wouldn't let it go. "So you're marrying strictly for money, not love?"

"Oh, I'll love him, all right. I'll love him to death, Fernando. He'll be my sweet patootie and die with a smile on his face."

Everyone fell out laughing over that.

When we had recovered and could breathe again, Jay said, "Where is Dennis? He's the only one missing from the group. I just realized that I haven't seen him since we got here."

"Who knows?" George said. "Who cares? I'm not asking, and I'm the lucky guy who gets to room with him. He wasn't in the hut when we returned from the game drive, and he's not here now. That's great. Fine by me. I don't care where he is or what he is doing. I hope he left."

"Left?" Jay said, "How could he leave? By taxi? Riding an elephant? Someone from the lodge would have to take him. We would know if he left. They would tell us. Is his stuff still here?"

"Yes."

"Well, then, so is Dennis."

"Maybe he's not feeling well," said Rose.

"He's not sick," George said. "If he was, he'd still be in the other bed in my hut. He's gone off somewhere, on one of his weird rambles. He does it all the time. I hate Dennis."

George was more than a little drunk.

"How could you hate Dennis, George?" Fernando asked. "You've only just met."

"I can. I do. I truly, truly hate Dennis."

George was trying to focus his eyes. His big red glasses slid down on his nose as he continued his impassioned speech, his voice rising. "I really hate Dennis. I hate what he says. I hate how he looks. I hate how he smells. When he's awake he says obnoxious things. When he sleeps, he snores louder than any man you ever heard. I *hate* rooming with him."

"But how do you really feel?" smiled Fernando.

"I hate you, too, Fernando, because you have a big room all to yourself."

"Yeah, and right next to the spa, too," Jay said. "How did you swing that, Fernando? I'm stuffed in with Sidney here."

I gave him a look. He had been making little digs at me all evening, probably because I had laughed at his clothes. He acts like a child when his feelings are hurt and he always gets mad if I laugh at his outfits. It's okay, of course, when he laughs at *my* clothes. But, outrageous as he looked in the Hemingway outfit, I really shouldn't have made fun of him. I know all too well how important his image is to him. Jay had probably spent two week's salary on the boots alone.

"My associate at the airline had to cancel at the last moment." Fernando said smoothly, finishing his glass. "So I am lucky, eh? But I am not a selfish man. I will swap rooms with you, Jay. Want to trade beds?"

He gave me a lazy smile.

"I will," George said.

"I didn't ask you, George," Fernando said. "I don't want to sleep with Dennis. I want to sleep with Sidney." He gave me a wicked grin as he rose and left the table.

"Is George sleeping with Dennis?" Connie asked.

"No!" George shouted.

Everyone shouted with laughter.

Just then, probably a good thing, David clapped his hands and announced that the escorts were ready to take us back to our huts. "Attention, ladies and gentlemen, may I have your attention, please. I'm afraid our *delightful* evening is drawing to a close. I had hoped to introduce you to the camp owner, Mr. van der Brugge, but something has undoubtedly delayed him. We will meet him another time. But tomorrow will be *thrilling*, what? A day of *rare excitement*, our first full day on safari. Morning will be here before you know it, darlings, so, *ta-ta* for now. Sweet dreams, my dears, and please be ready to leave promptly. I shall see you at dawn."

Everyone rose and said goodnight, except George, who announced that he was not ready to leave and made his way unsteadily toward the bar. Chase, Rich, Connie, and Jay decided to follow him. Fernando had already left.

David looked a bit miffed at their disobedience. He cleared his throat, trying to maintain his authority. "Those of you who would like to remain here for a quick nightcap may certainly do so if you choose. I don't think Willem will be closing the bar for a bit. But for those who are ready to turn in, please come this way. The guards are here to escort you. Remember, I shall look forward to seeing each and every one of you bright and early in the morning. Bright and early! Right, then. Cheerio, and may I wish you all a very good evening."

"Pip pip to you, too, David, old chap," slurred George. "I'm not going anywhere. Drinks all round, Willem. I'm not turning in. It's the shank of the evening."

"I'm with George," Jay said. "The night is young. Why are you shaking your head, Sid, and looking at me like a schoolteacher?"

"I just think I'm ready to go back to Hut No. 1, Jay. That's all. I don't care what you do. I'm ready to turn in. He's right. The game drive begins early."

"David is not my mother, and neither are you, Sidney. Did you know Fernando plays classical guitar? He went to get his guitar, and Chase and Rich and Connie and George here and I are going to crack open another bottle of wine and listen to him play it."

"Fernando brought a guitar on safari?"

"Yep. So you just run along like a good little girl, you and Tilda and Wendy, and go to bed when you're told. Nighty-night, party pooper, toodle-oo!"

"That's right, sugar," Connie said. "If you can't run with the big dogs, you better stay on the porch." They all laughed hysterically at that, and so I left. I wasn't really in a huff, but I was tired, and I hate it when Jay shows off at my expense.

He had been in one of his moods all evening, taking cute little potshots at me and encouraging the others to join him. I had made him feel foolish in his new outfit and so he was taking revenge. He doesn't do it often, but I've learned that when he does, the best thing to do is to get away from him for a while. By tomorrow, I knew, he would be remorseful and apologetic, trying to make up with me. I wouldn't make that easy for him.

"All of the guards have already left to escort other guests," Ronald told me at the door. "If you don't mind waiting here for just a few moments, Miss, I will call one of them back to take you to your room."

"That's quite all right, Ronald," said a deep voice behind me. "There is no need to call anyone. I will escort Miss Sidney Marsh to her quarters myself."

And that is how I came to be walking slowly through the African night with the tall, dark stranger from the Mount Nelson garden and Table Mountain path, Mr. Henrik van der Brugge, owner of Leopard Dance.

12

"Well, what do you think of South Africa, Sidney, now that you have left proper civilization behind in Cape Town?"

He took my arm and guided me down the steps and along the moonlit path.

My surprise at seeing him again and learning his identity had left me speechless.

"Is it as you expected?" he asked. "Do you like Leopard Dance?"

"I do, I really do. Very much. It is interesting, and so beautiful. I can see why you have chosen to live your life here."

"Can you now?" he said, smiling, "I wonder. And how do you know how I live my life? You know nothing about me. We've only just met. Careful there, love, don't trip."

He pointed his light on a protruding root in the dirt path, then slipped an arm around my waist as if to guide me around it.

"Well. I don't know how you l-live, of course," I stammered, "I don't really. I mean, I couldn't, could I? But I think it must be wonderful to own and run a camp like this, even with all the danger from the animals."

"It is very satisfying, that's what it is. And danger is always exhilarating. Always. Life here may seem somewhat monotonous, once you have settled into our routine, but I can assure you that it is not. Much more goes on here than is apparent. There is far more to Africa than lions and tourist camps."

Just then there was a rustle in the brush ahead. He stopped abruptly and pushed me behind him. Turning his light in the direction of the sound, he pulled a pistol from his coat pocket.

An antelope crossed the path on front of us. It paused to look at us for a long moment, and then bolted.

I didn't move, staying where he had placed me behind him until the sound of the fleeing animal died away.

"You can come out now. It's safe," he laughed, turning to face me, slipping the gun back in his pocket and switching off the light.

"You look beautiful in the moonlight, Sidney, and just as frightened as that gazelle. Relax, lady. There is nothing to fear when you are with me."

Isn't there? I thought. *I wonder.*

"Come," he said, putting his arm around my bare shoulders and guiding me on down the path. "Let's just stop in at your hut and leave a note for Mr. Wilson. Then I will take you to my house, offer you a nightcap, and show you how one really lives in Africa."

Yes! I thought. *Oh, yeah.*

But it was not to be. Not that night, anyway, because we were met at my door by Felix, with his big rifle.

"Henrik, there is trouble! You must come, come quick. They need you at the guard house." He burst into a torrent of Bantu.

"Thank you Felix," van der Brugge said in English. "I will be right with you. You go along now. Tell the others I am coming."

He unlocked my door for me as Felix ran back down the path. Then he smiled as he said goodbye, with a twinkle in those green eyes of his.

"Ah, well, dear Sidney, it seems that work must come before pleasure. As you heard, there seems to be a bit of a problem that I must handle. Duty calls. Go inside now, and lock the door. Get some rest. We will have to postpone your tour of my house until another time. Sleep well, love."

And with that he was gone, striding away into the darkness.

13

A snuffling sound woke me just before morning, and I lay quietly in the splendor of my luxurious bed, trying to decide if it was just one of Jay's exotic night sounds or a reason for alarm. I remained completely still, in the dark, listening.

There had been nothing quiet about Jay's return to our hut sometime after midnight. I had heard him singing on the path long before Felix helped him through the door. I pretended to be asleep, though that would have been difficult with him crashing around the room and cursing as he became tangled up in the mosquito netting while trying to climb into his bed.

In the predawn light I couldn't see Jay at all. The white mosquito nets draping my bed and his were too thick. I was reluctant to leave the warmth and comfort of my lovely nest to solve the mystery of the noise.

The snuffling sound grew louder. I decided that the sound was headed our way and seemed to be coming from right outside of Hut No. 1, on the river side.

Louder. Closer. And closer still.

Curiosity won out. I couldn't stand it. I had to know what was out there.

I had left the sliding wooden shutters closed and latched on the river side with the glass panels open so the evening breeze could pass through. The latch was stout. Jay had tested it when we first arrived, putting his full weight against it. I didn't think anyone or anything could open that lock from the outside.

I parted the netting, slipped out of bed, tiptoed across the floor, and peeped out through the louvers.

The eastern sky was getting lighter, and a big bull elephant was standing just to one side of our deck. His trunk made a slurping sound as he drank from a little pool of water in the mostly dry riverbed.

"Well, hello there, big boy," I whispered. "Are you going to come see us every morning? You must like Hut No. 1."

Awed by his size and the delicacy of his movements, I watched him until he quietly moved off down the riverbed, sipping from the puddles in the first gray light of dawn.

It is shocking how quietly an elephant walks. You would think they would make great thuds when they move because of their size, but that is not true. You only really hear thuds when they cross something like a wooden bridge. Elephants make crashing sounds, of course, when they break something by stepping on it, but their footsteps alone are quiet.

Now fully awake, I silently slid my drawer open and pulled pants and a fleece on over my pajamas. Then I unlocked the latch, softly slid the glass wall open, and stepped out onto the little deck. Our elephant friend had left us more large brown souvenirs, but he was no longer in sight. The only sounds now were birdcalls and the chatter of monkeys.

I stood quietly, watching and waiting to see if we would have more visitors. The dry riverbed seemed to be a main thoroughfare.

Peering into the early morning mist, I let my thoughts drift back to my evening stroll through the dark night with van der Brugge's arm around my shoulders. The mere memory of his nearness caused me to shiver. That stroll had ended way too soon, as far as I was concerned, when Felix called him away from my doorway.

The monkeys fell suddenly silent, bringing me out of my reverie. From up the riverbed, a beam of light from a flashlight appeared around the bend. I saw the lone figure of a man approaching. He walked quickly, but even so, he seemed to be looking for something or someone. He didn't point the light directly in front of him as he walked, but swung it side to side in constant motion.

I stepped back into the shadows just as the man passed below our deck. I didn't know who he was, but I had seen him before, in the moonlit garden of the Mount Nelson Hotel in Cape Town. I recognized him as the short, powerful black man who had been engaged in intense conversation with a certain tall handsome Afrikaner. This time, instead of an expensive suit, he wore camo.

Now what is he doing here? I thought. Does he work here? What is going on? Is he following us or are we following him? And who is he?

He walked with purpose, and was shining his powerful light along the riverbed and up into the overhanging tree branches. I watched in silence as he headed toward the center of camp. He was walking in the direction of the dining pavilion.

A sudden flash of light from Hut No. 2 next door startled the man and caused him to walk faster and move from the middle of the riverbed to the side. There the overhanging branches and vines mostly hid him from view. He paused for a while, standing still under the cover of the bank, as if trying to pinpoint the source of the flash. A peal of giggles and another flash confirmed the photographer's location, and for me, her identity. It was Wendy, with her ever-present camera and constant tittering.

The man moved quickly on, this time without his light, staying near the over-hanging earthen ledge. In seconds, he was out of sight.

Guess he didn't like Wendy taking his picture, I thought.

Hands gripped my shoulders and I jumped and shrieked and then swore. Jay, delighted at having succeeded in frightening me, shouted a laugh.

"Gotcha that time, didn't I, Sid? What did you think had you? A big gorilla or something? What do you think you are doing out here before sunrise anyway? Tai chi in the jungle?"

I didn't answer and he followed me back inside, sliding the glass panel closed and locking it.

"Are you still mad about last night Sidney?" he asked, now contrite. "I'm sorry if you are. I don't know what got into me. I didn't mean to hurt your feelings."

"You *bet* I am, funny boy. Yes, you scared the hell out of me. You *are* a big ape. And yes, you hurt my feelings last night. But that's okay because I'll get you back eventually. What goes around comes around, remember?"

"Well, you *ought* to be scared, girl, being out on the deck in the dark by yourself like that. What if it wasn't me? It could have been something big and bad, like that hungry leopard from last night. You're just lucky it was only me, Sidney. No telling what might have gotten you out there by yourself if I hadn't woken up and come to find you. I said I'm sorry. Don't be mad. I feel bad about you having to walk back to the hut all alone last night. Like I said, I don't know what got into me. I just got carried away."

"I didn't walk back alone."

"What?"

"I wasn't alone. Henrik van der Brugge walked me to the hut."

"The owner of Leopard Dance?"

"Yes, and he turned out to be the same guy I met on top of Table Mountain. Remember, the one you said I better be careful of?"

"No kidding? Well, that's still good advice, Sidney, because that also means that he is the guy you saw in the hotel garden with the dead man. We don't know how that came out, do we, only that it was foul play and definitely not a heart attack. My advice stands. You know what your mother would say, babe."

"I know, I know, the Marsh Curse—her catchall explanation of why the women on my father's side of the family always hook up with losers. I'm tired of hearing about that."

"Well, curse or no curse, most of the guys you pick out are the pits. Except, I guess, for sailor-boy, your ship captain, Captain Vargos. He *might not* be a loser."

"Never mind about him, Jay, that's none of your business. Boundaries, Jay, remember? Boundaries."

"Please. You are so touchy! Now don't be in a snit. We have our whole day ahead of us. Our coffee's coming and it will soon be time to head out."

"You said last night that you weren't going on any more game drives, Mr. Yellow Britches. I thought you were going to stay in camp from now on with Chase. He announced last night that he is not going on any more game drives, either. He said he was going to spend all the rest of his time guarding the pool and the spa."

"Well, that was last night, in the dark, with blood on the path and all. This is today. The sun's coming up. Daytime is okay. I can see stuff and run in the daylight. I just don't like that night business with wild animals sneaking around sniffing for you when you can't see them, hoping for a snack. And I still say that I do not like cocktails out in the open like that, either. I like my bars with walls. But it's almost morning now and I'm going on the game drive, okay? So give me a smile and let's get moving. It's almost time to leave."

⽊

We boarded the safari vehicles just after dawn. Jay rode in front by Vincent, with Connie and me next, and Fernando and George in the rear. Anthony was the game spotter for the day, riding in the usual seat on the left fender.

"No Dennis this morning either, George? Where's

Dennis?" I asked as we roared off into the mist.

George looked as if his head hurt. He was wearing big, dark sunglasses, although it was barely light. His hat was pulled down low over his glasses and the collar of his jacket was turned up against the cold. The trucks all had their headlights on. Our Land Rover was the lead vehicle leaving camp, with the others following.

"No Dennis today or last night either," he said. "He never came back. Thank you for asking. I said something this morning to the camp people but they were busy. No one seemed to know anything about him or be too concerned, so why should I be? He's not my responsibility. He doesn't like me any better than I like him. Maybe he asked to be moved to another room. Enough already. I don't want to think about Dennis. I don't want to spoil my morning."

I thought of the sight of Dennis, marching along the riverbed, clearly on a mission. Had he left camp then for good? Had he marched all the way back to the airport at Hoedspruit?

I wondered if the others shared my curiosity about Dennis's whereabouts. I didn't think so, because if they had any concerns about him, they weren't voicing them. Maybe George was right—Rebecca had reassigned him. That still didn't explain why he was absent from the morning game drive.

We all lapsed into silence. As before, conversation became difficult at the speed we were traveling because of the wind. We had left the camp drive and were rocketing down the main road. It was quite cold and everyone was huddled in their blankets.

There was nothing to see really, as we rushed through the crisp morning. I didn't know where we were headed or why we were going so fast. Vincent had not shared the plan with us, as usual, or even said hello. He certainly was not the chatty type.

Without warning, we lurched off the road, bounced through a shallow ditch, plunged onto a faint track through the thorn bushes, and then skidded down the sandy bank into the dry riverbed itself before rolling to a stop. The other vehicles followed.

"What the hell ..." Jay sputtered.

"Quiet," Vincent said, waving his arm to silence us. "Quiet everyone. Do not make a sound. We seek the leopard in his home. A spotter reported seeing him headed in this direction less than an hour ago."

"Oh God," Jay whispered.

Vincent put the Land Rover in gear and we slowly, silently, rolled forward, with all of us scanning the trees that overhung the river bank.

With the wheels barely turning, we crept along in the first light of dawn, looking upwards. Jerome used his powerful light on the branches, playing it back and forth, shining it first on one side, then the other.

Keeping one hand on the wheel, Vincent reached for his rifle with the other, laid it across his lap, and clicked off the safety.

I hoped Jay wasn't going to faint. He was certainly hyperventilating.

"The leopard waits and watches from the limbs of the trees," Vincent said softly. "When he sees something he likes, he leaps from the branch onto his prey and picks it."

Jay blanched and shuddered. I could tell he was terrified. I looked up at him, hoping he wasn't going to yammy all over the jeep. He looked as if he might.

"There," Jerome whispered, pointing ahead at a large tree. "He is there."

Jerome swung the light around, fixing on the branches ahead. Just above us and to our left in the crook of a tree lay a magnificent leopard. His tail, with its distinctive white tip, rested along the top of the thick branch and his paws hung down.

He was still, with his powerful muscles clearly visible beneath the tawny spotted skin. He was apparently sleeping, satiated by the kill he was guarding.

But his meal wasn't an antelope or a wildebeest or a warthog.

It was Dennis.

14

No one had been particularly fond of Dennis, but certainly none of us, not even George, wished him such a grisly fate.

Vincent gunned it back to camp, talking quietly into his radio the entire way.

Connie sobbed and howled and the rest of us just rode in grim silence, lost in our own thoughts. When we drove in through the gates, we passed van der Brugge's vehicle, speeding out of camp and headed into the bush.

After we unloaded, everyone scattered. Some of the group headed straight for the bar, but after talking for a little while with Rebecca, I went to Hut No. 1 for some aspirin to ease my monster headache.

Jay was already in the hut, pulling clothes out of the armoire and throwing them onto the bed. I stared at him.

"What are you doing?"

"What does it look like, Sidney? What do you think I'm doing? I'm packing. I'm leaving, getting the hell out of Dodge before I end up like Dennis. You can come with me or not, but I'm leaving."

"That is crazy, Jay. *Crazy.* I understand your fears of the big cats, especially after what's happened, but I do not understand this panic attack you are having. You are not going to end up like Dennis if you stay here."

I dug into my case for my aspirin, swallowed two, and stretched out on my bed and closed my eyes.

Jay wasn't buying that. He left off packing to stand beside my bed and rant.

"Yeah, well, I'm not so sure of that, Sidney. I'm not so sure of that at all, and neither are you. But I do know one thing, and I'm sure as hell of it. If I'm not here, then I *definitely* won't end up like Dennis. You can call me crazy all you want, but I refuse to be a tasty little treat for some big cat. I've had enough of this commune with nature stuff. I'm headed back to Cape Town."

"Jay, nothing is going to eat you," I said in an even voice, my eyes still closed. "Everyone is perfectly safe here if they follow the rules. Dennis didn't follow the rules and he paid for it."

"How would you know if Dennis followed the rules or not? You weren't hanging out with Dennis."

I opened my eyes and looked up at Jay. "No, but I know he didn't."

Jay moved around to his bed and started packing again, facing away from me, folding clothes and putting them in his suitcase. After a moment, he said, over his shoulder, "And just how could you know that?"

"Because I saw him leaving camp on foot, alone, that's why. He was walking by himself, up the riverbed, away from camp. That's how I know."

Jay stopped packing and perched on the bed. "When?"

I propped myself up on my elbows, pushing more pillows under my head. "Yesterday evening, just before the first game drive. I was out on the deck when I saw him, walking in the riverbed, away from camp. And he wasn't just out for a stroll. He was in a hurry and he looked as if he knew where he was going."

"Well, why didn't you stop him?"

"Seriously?"

"Okay. Well, maybe not. But why didn't you tell me?"

"Because you were in the shower and then you were all about your outfit and in a hurry to see everyone. Then I stayed way too long in the bubble bath and had to rush just to make the game drive. After that, with seeing the animals and everything, I forgot all about Dennis."

I slid off the bed, picked up the carafe, and poured myself a glass of water. After a sip, I continued. "Later, I wondered about it, because I knew he had lied to George and I couldn't imagine why. Dennis told George he was not going with us because he didn't feel well and was going to lie down and rest. But he didn't. He didn't take a nap at all. He left. As soon as George went to the bar, Dennis left, and I know that for sure because I saw him. Plus, Dennis was clearly no travel agent—any experienced agent could see that—so I wondered why he was pretending to be one."

"Yeah. I heard that goofy thing he said in the cable car about the Cunard ship."

"He made a lot of slips like that, Jay, and he was always wandering off from the group, even in Cape Town."

"So you think his death might not be random?"

I paused before answering. "Well, that's a big leap. I can't say that. But he for sure broke the camp rules for whatever reason and that got him killed. Whatever Dennis may have been, he wasn't stupid. He knew the risks of walking in the bush alone. He was told, just like the rest of us. Why he deliberately put himself in danger, or what he was doing in our group, posing as an agent, I don't know. But he had a reason, and it must have been a good one, for him to take a risk like that. It cost him his life."

Jay stepped over to the bar and poured two glasses of wine. His panic was subsiding. Jay is afraid of big bad cats, but not big bad people.

He handed me a glass. "Cheers. When you saw Dennis walking on the ditch, did you see anyone else?"

I took a sip. "No. He was alone."

"Did you see anyone following him?"

"No."

I thought back to the sight of Dennis marching along. I

had not seen anyone following him, but I hadn't been looking. I supposed that someone could have been following him, slipping along unseen under the cover of the overhanging bank. There was a lot of traffic outside our back door. That dry riverbed was beginning to turn into four-lane. First the animals, then Dennis, then the guy with the flashlight in the early morning. Where were they all heading?

Jay gave me a searching look. "Have you told anyone else about this?"

"Only Rebecca, just now. She thought it was strange, too. She said she thought Henrik, um, I mean Mr. van der Brugge might check into his background if there is an investigation."

Jay frowned. "What do you mean, if? There must be an investigation."

"Well, they will certainly look into it, Rebecca said, and the officials have been called. But she also said that they will likely just write it up as an accident. After all, he did wander out into the bush alone and unarmed, as far as anyone knows, and there are certainly wild animals out there that have to be respected. Everyone is well aware of that. It's a fact of life here."

Jay shuddered, but he was putting his stuff back into the wardrobe.

"I thought you were leaving."

"Well, I've changed my mind. Someone's got to look out for you, Sidney. And you need to keep your mouth shut about Dennis. We don't really know anything about any of these people. You are probably right. Dennis's death was probably caused by his own carelessness. But if it wasn't, if he was involved in something nasty that we don't know about, others may be involved as well."

He closed the cabinet drawers and sat down on the end of my bed again. "You are right about the rules, and you don't have to worry one minute about me breaking them. I'm sure not going strolling alone in the bush. But I think you also will need to keep your eyes and ears open from here on out, babe, and your mouth shut. This whole deal is really strange. I guess talking a bit to Rebecca was okay—she's sort of in charge of the camp—but don't tell anyone else about what you saw. That little walk Dennis took was not only fatal, it was fishy. If there is anything funny going on around here, neither one of us needs to be involved in it. We are only here for a few days. We need to steer clear. It's just not our problem."

He drained his glass. "Change into your swimsuit, sweetie, and grab a couple of towels. We're going to the pool to recover."

15

By mid-morning the pall cast over the camp by Dennis' gruesome end had basically lifted. It's probably a sad commentary on modern society or something, but that's how it was.

"I mean," Connie said, sipping a piña colada, "it's not like we really *knew* him."

"Stop making that straw gurgle," George said. "You don't have to drink every drop. They will bring you another one. And I must say that none of you realize how very traumatic this is for me. I knew Dennis well. I roomed with him, and I'm very sad about his death."

"Liar," Fernando said. "You are not sad, my friend. You are glad he is gone. You disliked him. You told us all that you did."

"Wrong. I didn't dislike him, it was more than that. I *loathed* him. I *despised* him. That doesn't mean I wanted him munched. I just wanted him to leave. To *go away*. And yes, I am glad he is gone, if you must know, but I am sad he was eaten."

"Can we just change the subject, people?" Jay said, "No more about Dennis, okay? Just talk about something else. Case closed."

"Wendy and Tilda suggested that we have a memorial service," I said. "But no one has stepped up, so I guess that's not happening. Are y'all okay with that?"

"Yes."

"Yes."

"Lord, yes."

"Sidney, get real," said George. "No memorial service. Enough about that. Not happening. Dennis is history. Now I'm going to the spa for a massage, guys. See you at lunch."

No one was in a mood for more conversation and the group soon drifted apart. Jay followed George to the spa; Connie went to have her nails done. Fernando pulled off his shirt, slipped into the pool, and started swimming laps. After a few moments of surreptitious admiration of *that* superb sight, I fell asleep in a hammock.

When I woke, I opened my eyes to find that everyone had disappeared except the chef, Willem, who was standing over me with a tray of snacks.

"Oh, sorry," he said, "I didn't mean to wake you. I didn't realize that you were sleeping. I apologize for disturbing you. But now that I have, would you like some hors d'oeuvres?"

He extended the tray of delightful little treats. I chose three and popped one into my mouth. "Thank you! This is wonderful!"

"Would you like more?"

"Actually, yes, I would, but I hate to be such a pig."

"Take all you want, Miss, there's no one else here to enjoy them."

I looked around, and he was right. Everyone seemed to have vanished, leaving us quite alone at the pool. I saw his frank appraisal of my red swimsuit, what little there was of it.

Willem set the tray down on the table and leaned against one of the carved wooden posts of the pavilion. He was an interesting-looking man, with a short, sturdy body, powerful arms, and round head with strands of blond hair falling into his sharp Dutch blue eyes. His deep tan was emphasized by his chef's whites.

"Do you mind if I smoke?"

"No, it won't bother me. There is a breeze."

"I do," Mabel's harsh voice rang out. She had just emerged from the library with an Afrikaans dictionary, of all things. She sat down in a lounge chair near the edge of the pool, out of the sun, and opened the book. "Please don't smoke."

Willem gave her a sharp look of annoyance but put the cigarette back in his pocket.

"Stay a moment, Willem," I said, patting the chair beside me. "Tell me how you came to be a chef in a game lodge."

"Thanks, I will," he said, shooting a glare over his shoulder at Mabel, who was making a great show of ignoring us, though she had positioned herself close enough to overhear our entire conversation. She was really beyond annoying.

"I have some time before we begin the luncheon service," he continued. "Everything is running very late today."

We spent several minutes watching some water buffalo drink from the waterhole while we chatted about the camp cuisine and the challenges of providing gourmet meals in a rustic setting. He spoke briefly of an early career in farming in Zimbabwe, telling his terrible story of how he was forced from his land like so many others.

"Cooking is not really what I planned to do, what I wanted to do. It was just what I *could* do. I grew up on the land, had worked the land all my life, like my father before me. After they took my farm, I had nothing. Nothing except my car and what little I could carry in it. We left Zimbabwe in the middle of the night and bribed our way across the Limpopo into South Africa, feeling lucky to be alive. I cast about for a bit, taking odd jobs so we could eat. I was always handy in the kitchen, so one thing led to another. I got a bit of training, Henrik gave me this job, and here I am."

"What sort of man is Henrik? Is he a good boss?"

"Yes, he is. He's fair. He doesn't skimp on things. He pretty much gives me free rein in how I run the kitchen, isn't always checking behind me, as long as the guests are happy. He's actually not here much. He also has lots of cash, so he doesn't have to watch his pennies like most of us."

"Well, you are very good at running your kitchen, Willem. Your food is delicious. Are the dishes you prepare mostly South African or are they from Zimbabwe?"

He seemed pleased by the praise. His blue eyes lost a bit of their wariness.

"A little of both," he replied. "Some of them are Dutch, family recipes. My ancestors were original Voortrekkers, Boers who fled the British in ox wagons. Actually, now that I think of it, the bulk of the dishes that make up my menus here in camp are from recipes I used in Zimbabwe."

"Do those require special ingredients? Isn't it difficult to get things from Zimbabwe, under the present regime?"

He smiled, but the blue eyes had hardened again. "It would be, yes, if I had to get my supplies there. Quite difficult. I could send for things, I suppose, but the bribes I would have to pay would be more than the cost of the food. Luckily, I don't have to. I can find all I need right here. I would never personally try to go grocery shopping across that border. I can't set foot in Zimbabwe. I expect there's still a price on my head in some circles in Harare."

Willem was certainly the most interesting chef I had ever met. I wondered just how bad life had been for this man. Undoubtedly, there was much more in his experience that he had left unsaid.

"You have truly an amazing story, Willem. But earlier, you said 'we' left Zimbabwe. Who else came with you?"

"My wife."

That surprised me. I had thought he was single. No one had been introduced as his wife.

"Oh. I haven't met her," I said, wondering who she might be. "Is she here in camp?"

"She is not. Cast out, living by our wits ... It was too much for her. She couldn't take it. She left me for another, a rich man. But later, she left him, too."

As he said this, his sharp blue eyes held a look of grim satisfaction. "I'll never be as poor as that again. Never. I can promise you that. I'll never forget those days. I've done pretty well for myself since then. I've managed to save a bit of cash, even bought into this operation. I only have a small bit, nothing like Henrik, but my interest will grow in time."

Willem stood and picked up the tray. "Well, then," he said, "that's more than enough of my sad story. I must get back to the kitchen. Lunch will be served soon."

An odd sound interrupted his narrative, a deep, rough sound, like a saw cutting wood.

I glanced in the direction of the sound. "What is that noise?" I asked. "Are they building onto the kitchen?"

"No," he laughed, "it's only Sheba, Mr. van der Brugge's leopard. That's one of the sounds she makes. Henrik raised her from a cub. Lions killed her mother."

"A leopard? Really? What a strange pet! Aren't you afraid of her?"

"No," he laughed. "I like her a lot. She keeps me company. I help him train her. I work with her a bit every day. Sheba is as well trained as a wild cat can be."

We heard the strange, sawing cough again.

"Her main enclosure is just behind the kitchen," he continued. "He has another for her at his house. Sheba sleeps most of the day and is usually pretty silent. That rough cough means that something has disturbed her. Perhaps she longs for a mate, or for her lunch like everyone else. And speaking of lunch, I really must go now."

He paused in the doorway, giving me a sharp look. "You should ask your friends for a report on tonight's meal. I am serving roast springbok with a wild mushroom and claret reduction," he said, watching me closely with his sly blue eyes. "I understand you will not be dining with us."

"What? Oh, no, that's a mistake. I will be at the table with my friends tonight. I just skipped breakfast because I was sad and didn't feel like eating after what happened. I'm okay now. I'll have lunch, and I will be here tonight as well. Where else would I be?"

"At Mr. van der Brugge's table. In his house. You are to be his guest for a private dinner tonight after the evening game drive. His only guest. At least, that's what he personally ordered, not an hour ago. He asked me to send his invitation for a private dinner to your room and that has already been delivered. I was also asked to plan a very special dinner. I hope you enjoy it."

I was speechless.

"Right then, I'm off to the kitchen."

He gave me a sly smile and walked away.

16

The invitation, handwritten on paper imprinted with the snarling leopard logo, was on my bed when I walked into Hut No. 1.

The only problem was that it had been opened, and someone large and redheaded was reading it. Aloud.

> Dear Sidney,
> Please join me for dinner this evening at my home after Sundowners. Nigel, my driver, will bring you.
> —Henrik

"Excuse me, I believe that is mine," I said, snatching it out of his hands. "And get off my bed with your shoes. Mess up your own bed."

"Well, well, well, little Miss Secrets," he said, not budging an inch, but at least nudging the shoes off onto the floor. "Don't be so huffy. It was pushed under the door and it wasn't sealed. Confession time, Sidney. Just what did you do to rate this little treat? Or what are you planning to do? Tell Uncle Jay, sweetheart. I won't breathe a word to anyone, I promise."

"Yeah, right, you bet. Not until you needed a funny story over drinks. Where I have dinner or with whom is none of your business or anyone else's, for that matter. And that envelope was addressed to me, not you, my nosy friend. You had no business opening it."

He sat up, laughing at me, and as always, enjoying my

indignation. "Are you in a snit, babe? A real one?"

"Probably not, but you shouldn't have opened my mail. Boundaries, remember? We need some boundaries here."

"When have we ever had boundaries, Sidney?" He got off the bed and padded over to my closet. "Now, what are we going to wear?"

When Gabriel blows the trumpet, Jay is not going to heaven unless they have designer robes. He loves a logo more than anything, so his dive into my closet for a good dinner dress was beyond disappointing for him. He came up empty. Big surprise.

"This stuff you brought is pitiful. I guess you're stuck with wearing that black thing or the red sundress again. Really, sweetie, when we get back home, I'm taking you shopping."

"Great! I would love that! Does that mean you are paying?"

"Of course not," he said as he headed to the shower to begin his evening ritual, "I'm just offering my expert advice. You know I never have any money. Neither do you, really. What you truly need is a sugar daddy to buy you a nice wardrobe. Take a lesson from Connie. What about van der Brugge? Play your cards right tonight and he might buy you a dress or two. If that doesn't work, there's always Silverstein. He's got a ton of money."

He closed the bathroom door just in time. My aim was off. The shoe just barely missed his head.

⚓

Jay was belting out a show tune in the shower, so I almost didn't hear the faint tapping at the door.

I opened the front door, looked out, saw no one, and closed it. But the insistent tapping continued, and I finally realized that it came from the back door, the sliding glass one in the window wall on the river side.

I pushed aside the louvered wooden shutters and saw Winsome, the night maid, standing on the deck, waiting impatiently for me to unlock and open the glass.

"Winsome! I'm sorry. I didn't realize you were there. I almost didn't hear you. You should have knocked or called out, instead of tapping. Please, come in."

"No. Miss," she whispered, "I can stay only a moment before I am missed. I cannot come in. Please, step outside. I must speak with you, quickly."

She seemed very nervous, her head constantly swiveling, her eyes darting back and forth as she scanned the paths, the brush, and the riverbed.

I stepped out onto the deck, sliding the wooden shutters closed behind me. "Well, here I am. What is it? You are upset, Winsome. Is something wrong?'

"Tonight, Miss," she whispered. "Tonight I speak with Ingwe. He tells me that you are coming for dinner at the big house. Fine dinner, you know the dinner I mean, with Mr. van der Brugge."

What is going on here? Jungle drums beating out Sidney's dinner plans?

"Yes," I said with a smile, "I have been invited to have dinner tonight at Mr. van der Brugge's house. Did you say Ingwe? Is that a nickname?"

"Ingwe is a bad man, Miss. You must stay away from Ingwe, Miss. I tell you, stay away from him. You have been kind to me, so I come to warn you. Do not spend time with him. Do not talk to him. Do not believe what he says. Only harm comes from Ingwe. That is all I can say but you must listen, must believe. I know him. Stay away from Ingwe."

And with that she was gone, melting away into the trees and brush lining the riverbank. She was gone, but her warning remained. I didn't know what to think.

The door slid open behind me. Jay stood there in his bathrobe. "Sidney, I heard someone talking. Who was that?

Was that Winsome? What did she want?"

I told him what she had said.

"That's odd, but I don't know how much stock I would put into it. He's not exactly my type, but I have to say that van der Brugge doesn't seem at all sinister to me. I wouldn't let Winsome's warning stop me if I really wanted to go."

"Well, I'm not. I'm definitely still planning to go. I really want to see that house. It's supposed to be fabulous, and I'm a big girl. I'm not afraid of van der Brugge. After all, he is our host. What is there to be afraid of? After all, the whole world seems to know where I'll be dining this evening and with whom. Still, it is strange that she would sneak up here like that with a mysterious warning."

"Winsome likes you. I can tell."

"Yes, and I like her. I asked her what it is like to live here, far from the city, with so much beauty and danger all around. She was born near here. Her grandfather was a shaman. She told me all about her life and her family. She loves her job here, but she has ambition. She wants to move away to Johannesburg."

Jay scanned the thicket where Winsome had gone, as if checking to be sure she was gone. "This cryptic warning of hers is strange."

I followed him back into the hut, watching as he slid the glass shut and bolted it. "It is. Totally unlike her. She's usually calm, smiling, and serene."

"From what I overheard, she wasn't calm tonight."

He headed toward the bathroom to finish getting dressed, then paused in the doorway and turned back to me as if some light bulb had just gone off in his head.

"Oh, *I know* what it is, hon. *I know.* She sees you as *competition.* She probably just has the hots for him, too."

"What was that you said, Jay? What was that word?"

"You mean 'hots'?"

"No. I mean 'too.' I do not 'have the hots' for Henrik van

der Brugge. I'm just going to dinner and to see the house. That's all."

He laughed as he closed the bathroom door, "Whatever you say, Sid, whatever."

⊁

The evening game drive was cancelled that night for obvious reasons. The pre-dinner sundowners were being served instead at a hippo pool downriver. Our regular schedule, Rebecca told us, would resume in the morning.

When the bell rang, we went to the pickup point outside the welcome pavilion but had to wait until the entire group was present before boarding the vehicles. Everyone was scheduled to leave together.

So we were all delayed in departing by Wendy and Tilda, who were late. They finally came rushing up the path, clearly upset.

Wendy was in tears. "All of my pictures, gone. Every last one of them."

"What happened?" asked Connie. "Who took them?"

"Who would want them?" muttered George.

"Monkeys!" Tilda shrieked. "Nasty little thieving monkeys. They got in our hut and pulled out all our things, ate all our biscuits, pooped all over the room—even in our beds—and broke Wendy's camera."

"Now I don't have any record at all of our lovely trip," Wendy sobbed. "All of my beautiful pictures, gone."

"How did they get in?" asked Rose. "Didn't you lock your door?"

"We each thought the other had locked it, but we must have been mistaken. We must have left it open."

The blond heads of the women bobbed in agreement to each other and then to us.

"Was anything taken?" Fernando asked Wendy.

"Only the memory card from the camera," she replied. "Those little boogers broke my camera all to pieces. We found most of the bits, but not the memory card. They must have taken it with them when they ran out. We looked everywhere but we didn't find it."

"The monkeys ran out screeching when I came in," Tilda added. "Scared us silly! All except one, who was up on the ceiling fan, chattering. Felix had to chase him out with the broom."

Wendy sobbed. "The only thing taken was the record of my memories."

Rebecca clapped her little hands.

"Ladies and gentlemen, it is time to leave. Please take your accustomed seats in the vehicles."

"You betcha," George said. "Enough of this monkey business. We're out of here!"

17

The setting for the Sundowners cocktail party at the hippo pool was totally amazing. It didn't look real. It looked like a scene from a movie. A lavish, big budget Hollywood movie. We arrived at the water's edge just before sunset.

The party was set up on a gently sloping grassy patch leading down to the river. This section of the river was deep, with plenty of water, despite the fact that the rains had not yet arrived. Armed guards stood on the perimeters to keep us safe, so for once, Jay relaxed. As time went on, his fear of the animals was subsiding. By the time we got back home I was sure he would be eager to return to Africa.

Tables covered with smooth white linens and trays of wine and hors d'oeuvres had been set up at one end of the hippo pool, close to the water but far enough back so as not to disturb the animals. Fresh flowers in glass bowls and tea lights in crystal holders centered each table. The idyllic scene was suffused in that golden late-afternoon sunlight that cinematographers sometimes refer to as "the magic hour." The water was still, reflecting the breathtaking scene.

"Like a mirror," I said. I couldn't take my eyes off it, or the uncanny way the water reflected the colors of the sky.

"*Spieël*," Mabel said.

"What?" said George.

"*Spieël*. That's Afrikaans for mirror."

"Oh. Okay. Thanks for sharing."

Mabel glared at George and walked away. Mabel had had her long nose in an Afrikaans phrase book she had borrowed from the camp library, so she had a leg up on the rest of us in translating words from the old Dutch language.

We were served flutes of sparkling wine and helped ourselves from a beautiful display of cheese and fruit. Waiters passed silver trays of delightful treats—mushrooms stuffed with crabmeat, marinated artichokes and prawns, tiny skewers of grilled eland. The fine wine, food, and setting were having the desired effect. Everyone relaxed and enjoyed the evening.

We received an unexpected bonus in the arrival of a magnificent black rhino at the far end of the pool. It was almost as if the Hollywood director in my imagination had shouted "Cue the rhino!" The timing of the appearance of the great armored beast was that perfect, and that special. I felt bad for Wendy. The rhino's appearance made her mourn the loss of her camera even more.

David was frantically motioning for all of us to gather round. For this special occasion he had added a pith helmet to his khaki safari garb.

"Gold braid, military jodhpurs and some Boer War medals will be next," Jay murmured. "Just wait and see."

I think he was jealous.

"Please remain near the tables and try to speak softly," David stage-whispered. "This is *ripping* good fortune. A rhino sighting is a *rare excitement* to be *relished* and *remembered*."

"He's rrreally rrrrolling those Rs again," Jay said so softly that only I could hear.

"What if he charges us?" asked Connie. "Should we run for the cars or just try to hide?"

"He will not charge," said Vincent. "We are too far away. He likely does not even know we are here. His eyesight is poor and we are downwind of him."

"I know that's right," said Connie, wrinkling her nose.

"Why is it rare and unusual to see a rhino?" asked Jay. "I thought South Africa had tons of rhinos."

"Because they're killing them all, that's why," snapped Mabel in her rude way, as if Jay was the stupidest man on the planet. "Poachers kill them for their horns. South Africa has a little over 20,000 rhinos, the most of any country in the world. That seems like a lot, but just last year poachers killed a record number, over 455 of those. The rhinos have been wiped out by ninety percent in the last forty years. Ninety percent! Where have you been that you don't know that, Mars?"

Jay ignored her, concentrating instead on refilling his wineglass. I just hoped he wasn't going to pour it over her head. He was in full sympathy with the plight of the rhinos, but not with Mabel. Almost every word she said irritated him. He really just couldn't stand her, but then again, neither could anyone else. It wasn't so much what she said as how she said it. Mabel had an unfortunate way of speaking that irritated everyone. I could see Jay steaming.

But I was reassessing my feelings toward her. If Mabel was kindhearted enough to be concerned about the rhino, she might not be so bad after all.

"Why do they want the horns?" asked Connie. "You can't eat them and they are not very pretty."

"For money," Fernando said. "Big money. Powdered rhino horn sells for as much as cocaine, and for more than gold. It is a very lucrative business, operated by organized cartels."

"It's wicked," said Mabel. "They paralyze them with tranquilizer guns, then hack off their horns with a machete or a chainsaw and leave them to die."

"Amazing to learn that she has compassion for any living creature," muttered Jay. "She hates people, but rhinos turn her on. Who knew?"

"But isn't it hard to kill a rhino?" asked Connie. "I mean, they are so big and all and their hide is so thick. I don't think it would be easy."

"It is easy enough with a high-powered rifle," said Fernando. "These poachers are not hunting with spears and popguns. They have criminal networks behind them. It is big business and they are well-supplied and financed. They use helicopters, night-vision equipment, high-powered rifles with silencers and scopes, and tranquilizers. They are skilled and very quick. They bring them down, harvest the horn, and are gone in five minutes. Sometimes they don't kill them, only tranquilize them long enough to hack off the horn, then leave them to bleed to death."

"That's so brutal," Jay said.

"Yes, it is," replied Fernando. "And as Zimbabwe has become more lawless, poachers and arms smugglers have an easier time of it, working back and forth across the borders."

"But why doesn't someone stop them," Connie said, "if everyone knows what's happening? What about the police? Isn't it against the law?"

"Yes, of course. The rhino is supposed to be protected and safe within the national parks. But the park rangers are outnumbered and working over a large area, and some officials have been known to look the other way. A gift of money can go a long way for a poor man and his family."

"But what do they do with the horn?" Jay asked. "How is it used? Do they smoke it?"

"No." Fernando laughed. "The big market is China and Vietnam, where for hundreds of years it has been an ingredient in traditional medicines. They believe it cures many things, from cancer to impotency."

"Does it?" asked George, suddenly interested. He had been looking bored with the conversation up to that point.

"No, silly," blurted Mabel. "It is a complete fraud. Western scientists have tested rhino horn for medicinal value and there is none."

"You seem to know a lot about the effects of rhino horn, Fernando," said George. "Have you personally tried it?"

"No, my friend, but perhaps you should. It is totally unnecessary for me."

"Zing!" said Jay. "He got you that time, George."

"It is no laughing matter, and only ignorant fools like you and George would think so," shouted Mabel. "If I saw even a hint of anything like that going on, I would report it immediately to the highest authority. And I would not rest until the perpetrators were punished."

Mabel's shrill voice had risen to such a fever pitch that it even attracted the attention of the bored guards. I saw them exchange glances.

For the first time on the trip Mabel had everyone's attention, so she climbed up on her soapbox and spent the rest of the time preaching to anyone who would listen until it was time to leave. Even those in total agreement with her about the rhino poaching also knew that she had managed to spoil a splendid evening.

"Listening to her makes me want to root for the other side." George said. "That woman is so unbearable. I wish a poacher would just buzz over in his helicopter and take her out instead of the rhino."

"Hush, George," I said, "everyone can hear you. Mabel will hear you."

"I hope she does. Maybe then she'd be insulted enough to never speak to me again. That's what I would really like."

"Well at least she wants to help the poor animals," said Connie.

"Connie, George is right," Jay said. "Animals or no animals, that woman is utterly horrible. Poison. I can't stand her. I feel so sorry for poor Rose. If I were staying in the same room with Mabel, I think I would just suddenly snap and choke her to death with my bare hands just to get her to shut up. Imagine having to listen to that 24/7."

"Excuse me, Miss Marsh," Vincent interrupted. "Nigel, Mr. van der Brugge's driver, is here to collect you for dinner.

Please come this way. He is waiting in the car."

"Well, well, well," said Jay. "Now isn't that nice? Off you go to the fancy dinner with the big man in the big house, Sidney, while we're stuck here with the lovely Mabel. Even the rhino's left. He couldn't take her voice, either. Have a good time, sweetie, and remember, when you get back, I expect a full report."

18

The house was huge, elevated, and surrounded on all sides by a wide verandah. The long driveway leading up to it was lined on either side by an impressive row of yellowwood trees.

He stood in the shadow at the top of the stairs, watching me as I ascended the double stairway in the gathering dusk. He was so still and silent that I was startled when he spoke.

"Hello, Sidney," he said, stepping forward to greet me, taking my hand in his. "Welcome to my home. Please, come inside. What will you have to drink?"

He led me through a stately entrance hall into a large and beautiful room, with massive carved pillars of dark wood that supported the exposed beams of the roof. Floor to ceiling windows—framed by long white silk curtains rustling gently in the breeze—were open to the verandah. Handsome yellowwood and stinkwood furniture, much of it clearly antique and valuable, filled the room, reflected in the gleaming dark wood of the floors. The walls were the color of old ivory and lined with original works of art and antique mirrors.

He handed me a glass of wine, looking amused at my obvious wonder at this palace set in the middle of the bush.

"You are asking yourself why I live alone here like this, in such splendid isolation."

"I am, yes. Your home is magnificent. So much of this furniture is antique."

"Family pieces. My family history here dates back to the Dutch East India Company."

"Really? Willem told me his ancestors were Boers. Were yours as well?"

"No. Entirely different group. The history of South Africa is long and complicated, Sidney, involving many different people, many different groups."

"But all very interesting."

"Interesting, yes. Dramatic, and often tragic. It's a long story, darling, one that I will tell you some day perhaps, but I did not invite you here to talk about myself. I want to know instead about you, what your life is like, and what brings you to Africa."

I was just about to reply when I sensed motion on my right.

A full-grown leopard had just entered through the tall, floor-length open window and was standing very still, watching me, silent and motionless, not twenty feet away. Only its tail was moving, the distinctive white tip twitching.

I froze, staring at the big cat.

"Ah, Sheba, you have come to greet our guest. Sidney, this is Sheba, my pet leopard. I raised her from a cub, after her mother was killed by lions. Don't worry, she will not harm you. She is only curious. We don't have many guests. Please, be seated. Here, close to me, so she will know you mean no harm. Sheba is very protective. Relax. You'll be fine."

I sat carefully next to him on the leather sofa facing the fireplace but there was no way I could relax with a live leopard in the room. Henrik put his arm around my shoulders. A low fire crackled and popped in the fireplace under the great mantel. It should have been romantic, I guess, but as I watched the cat pace, all I could think about was Dennis.

The leopard circled the sofa as I sat stone still beside Henrik. Apparently deciding I was okay, she stretched lazily in front of the fire before settling on the hearth rug. Then she began licking her paws, much like an ordinary housecat.

"You see, she senses that you are a friend. Don't be afraid of her. She is really quite harmless."

"Is she? Does she still have her teeth and claws or did you have those removed?"

"Oh, no. I would never do that. She has her full arsenal. I would never deprive her of the joy of the hunt."

I sipped my wine, fighting the urge to drain it. My nerves were strung tight by this man and his cat. It's not every day that you have drinks with a leopard ... or with a man equally as handsome as his beast, and likely as dangerous. I thought of Jay and what he would do and say if he were here. I recalled Winsome's warning.

With a broad smile and a little bow, van der Brugge touched his glass to mine.

"To Africa, Sidney, and to you. I'm glad you like Sheba. I believe she likes you as well. I will take you with us sometime when she hunts and let you see what she can do. She is magnificent."

The cat yawned just then, proving that she did indeed have all of her teeth. Then she rose, stretched, and padded back through the curtains, disappearing into the darkness beyond the porch.

I exhaled, realizing that I had been holding my breath for quite a long time.

"Mr. van der Brugge—"

"Henrik."

"Henrik, then," I began again. His arm tightened around my shoulders. He was watching me carefully, an amused smile on his lips and in his dark green eyes. I almost lost my train of thought. I took a sip of wine.

"Go on."

"Well ... who named this place 'Leopard Dance'?"

"I did, darling, I did. In the very beginning, I named it. I am fascinated with leopards. Though terribly dangerous, they are also beautiful. And the beast is a self-sufficient, solitary creature. Like you. And like me. *Ingwe*, they call the cat. That is a Zulu word. It means both king and leopard. One must be careful in the presence of *Ingwe*."

Once again, Winsome's words came to mind.

"Then there may be truth in what your drivers say."

"And what is that, my love? What do my drivers say?"

"They say, 'He who dines with the leopard is liable to be eaten'."

He laughed then, and smiled down at me, pulling me closer.

"That's an old native saying, my dear, and it may be true. One must be very careful with a leopard."

He smiled again. I shivered, thinking again of Dennis.

A white-coated servant appeared in the doorway and bowed, saying something in Bantu.

Van der Brugge answered him, also in Bantu, then rose and took my hand, pulling me to my feet. "Come now, Sidney, Timothy says that our dinner is waiting."

He led me into a splendid, candlelit dining room, and seated me on his right at a stately table overlaid in crisp damask and set with delicate china, heavy silver, and sparkling crystal. A massive arrangement of birds of paradise in a huge silver bowl dominated the center of the table. Another white-coated servant placed before us plates of prawns topped with a remoulade sauce, passed a basket of crisp herbed toast, and poured more wine.

"This is lovely," I said. "Thank you for inviting me."

"The pleasure is all mine, my dear. I'm very glad you are here." He smiled. "I've wanted to dine with you ever since we met in Cape Town. Our chance meeting was quite a coincidence, wasn't it? At the time, of course, I had no way of knowing that the lady who accosted me in the Mount Nelson garden and jumped into my arms on Table Mountain would be my guest at Leopard Dance. Your group's visit was scheduled weeks ago, but I didn't realize that you were a part of it until I saw you with the group on Table Mountain. Is this your first visit to Africa?"

"No. I visited Kenya once and have seen some of Northern Africa. But this is my first visit to South Africa."

"Not all business? Surely some of these trips must be for pleasure."

I smiled. "Actually, my business *is* pleasure, most of the time. I escort groups of tourists on trips throughout the world. It's great for me because I get to see places I could never afford to visit on my own. I love to travel."

"But isn't it rather confining, being stuck with these groups all the time?"

"Well, yes, it can be, but I don't mind. I like my clients. Most of them are really nice people who enjoy seeing the world as much as I do. It's a wonderful job."

"Well, we at Leopard Dance are very pleased to welcome you and your associates to South Africa. Everyone is happy to have you here. We need your business. Tourism remains the lifeblood of our country and, as a businessman, I hope that your group's little introductory tour will be the beginning of a mutually beneficial relationship. As for myself, I will look forward to personally introducing you to my private Eden."

His pitch was interrupted by shrill rock music blaring loud and then louder. The sound was coming from the front of the house, from the front drive. Van der Brugge flung his napkin on the table, pushed back his chair, and headed to the door to investigate. The volume of the music, which had been steadily increasing, was now really shrieking.

"If you'll excuse me for a moment, Sidney, I'll just try to find out ..."

At that moment, there was a loud boom and crash at the front of the house and sounds of glass breaking. The house shook, setting the prisms of the chandelier tinkling.

Van der Brugge ran through the entry hall toward the sound. I followed, as did the waiter, the cook, and all the kitchen helpers. He flung open the massive front door, and we all froze in shock at the sight.

A silver Porsche convertible had crashed into the wide front steps. The car rested halfway up the stairway, its front end crumpled and air bag deployed. Smoke was beginning to rise from the engine.

The driver, a curvy platinum blonde in a low-cut dress, was apparently unhurt, laughing, and quite drunk.

"Hello, Henrik," she shouted, slurring. "I heard you were having a fancy dinner tonight and thought I'd join you. Gonna introduce me to your little hottie?"

"Who is that woman?" I asked Timothy as van der Brugge ran down the steps toward the car. "Is she a friend of Henrik's?"

"No, Miss," said Timothy. "She is not his friend. She is his wife."

19

"His *wife*?" shrieked Jay. "Really, his *wife*? *No kidding*?" He was laughing so hard his big shoulders were shaking.

I was back in Hut No. 1, sitting cross-legged on my bed, telling him all the details of my dramatic evening. Nigel had driven me back home after the fiasco that my big romantic dinner had become.

"That is *hilarious*. His wife? You really know how to pick 'em, don't you, Sid? I think your mom is right about that Marsh Curse. You really do have terrible luck with men."

My mother has this notion that all the women on my father's side of the family are doomed to have bad romantic relationships. She calls it the Marsh Curse. She may be right. My dad has seven sisters, and Mamma bases her curse theory on the fact that all my aunts' love lives are marred to a greater or lesser degree by disaster. They have experienced multiple false promises, marriages, divorces, annulments, jiltings, and cons. Only one sister, Aunt Minnie, has managed to escape, and my mother says that's only because she is too proper and prim to have ever had a beau.

I've had my share of unfortunate experiences with unsuitable boyfriends. And those guys, plus the lack of a ring on my left hand, have convinced Mamma that I'm headed down the same bewitched path as my aunts. As a front row spectator in the ongoing tragicomedy that is my love-life, I think Jay agrees with Mamma.

"It was not hilarious, Jay. It was *awful*. He peeled her out of that car, and before I could leave, she spotted me and started screaming. She called me all sorts of names and then lit into him. By that time the servants had managed to take charge of her and were hustling her into the house. Then van der Brugge stuffed me into his car, apologizing all over the place, and told Nigel to drive me home. He tried to insist that she is his *ex-wife,* not his wife, but I don't think I believe him. His staff all called her his wife. Winsome was right. I should have listened to her warnings."

"Yeah, you should have, Sidney, and I must have been asleep at the switch myself. I told you to go. I thought he was okay. I should have picked up on that guy. He fooled me, and I'm pretty good at spotting phonies. I hope the faulty judgment that plagues the Marshes isn't rubbing off on me."

"Jay," I said, leaning forward on my elbows and staring at him intently as he lounged, propped up by pillows on the opposite bed, "before the evening exploded, he was making this pitch about being grateful for our business, needing our business. Something about all that was beginning to really bother me."

"Why was that, Sweetie?"

"Well, Jay, where do you suppose van der Brugge is getting all his money? The tour operators I've met don't usually live like this guy does. From what he said, he's self-made. As far as I've been able to tell, and from what he said tonight, this safari lodge is his only current business. Now this place apparently does well—it's well-maintained and staffed—but could a safari lodge really bring in that kind of cash? You know it must cost a lot just to run this place. I can't think that the profit margin is huge, even when fully booked, and right now there's hardly anyone here but us. Yet everything about the man suggests serious money. You should have seen that house, Jay. I mean, that house and all the stuff in it must have cost a fortune."

"Yeah, and don't forget the airstrip and the plane, too.

You're right. It doesn't add up. The rates at this camp are about average. They're not astronomical at all, and David told us that the lodge is not fully booked, even in high season. Maybe he's got something going on the side, something shady. There's a lot of slippery stuff that happens across and near these borders. You heard what Fernando said."

"Yes, and Mabel, too."

"Let's just leave Mabel out of any discussion, Sidney. I don't like her any more than George does, and he is about ready to murder her."

"Mabel can be annoying, Jay—I have to agree with y'all on that, and I don't like her insensitivity toward people—but I do agree with her on some subjects. What she said about the rhinos was right. "

"I know, but I don't care. Right or not, whatever she's for, I'm against. Hold on now, don't get huffy. Relax. I'm not against the rhino. Just against Mabel. She's poison. I'm sorry, but that's just how she affects me."

There was a knock on the door then, and Felix's voice forced me up and off of the bed. I opened the latch, and Felix stepped into the room, bearing a lovely dinner tray and a bottle of wine. He leaned his big rifle against the wall and set the heavy tray down on the table by the sliding glass wall on the river side. He waited as I opened the card.

> Sorry your dinner with the boss didn't turn out so well. I hear you've met the lovely wife. I expect this might be welcome. Bon Appétit!
> —Willem

"Now isn't that nice," I said. "Felix, please thank Willem for me. This is very kind of him, and I will certainly enjoy it. And thank you for bringing it to me."

Even as I was thanking him, I wondered how word of the debacle at van der Brugge's house had spread so quickly. Eyes and ears truly were everywhere, it seemed. My pals were going to get a real kick out of this story. Connie would be sharing it over cocktails for years. I couldn't blame her. Travel agents can be a gossipy bunch, and they love a good story. A tale like this one would be irresistible.

"Please do not set the tray outside when you finish, Miss, because of the animals. Ring the bell and someone will come pick it up, or just leave it inside until morning. Is there anything else you need this evening?"

"Oh, thank you, no, Felix. This is wonderful. Thank you." I didn't give him a tip. As with cruise ships, Leopard Dance had a strictly cashless policy. Tips for services were paid at the end of the stay.

"Very well, then, Miss. Goodnight."

"Ooooh, this is yummy!" Jay popped a samosa—a deep-fried potato pastry—in his mouth.

The door hadn't closed behind Felix before Jay was sampling. Besides the samosa appetizer, the tray held a steaming plate of bobotie, a South African curried meat casserole, bread, a salad, and a dessert assortment of fruit and cheese with some little spiced wine cookies called soetkoekies.

South Africa has marvelous cuisine, with unusual dishes that reflect the various nationalities of her settlers and explorers. Bobotie is a traditional dish that probably has its early origins in Indonesia or Malaysia. It was served, as it customarily is, with geelrys, a slightly sweet, yellow rice dish, and a side of mango chutney. Bobotie is comfort food and it tasted great. After my dinner party from hell, comfort was exactly what I needed. Jay was digging into my dish with the dessert spoon.

"Stop that," I said. "Leave my tray alone, piggy pants. You've already had dinner. I haven't, remember? I'm starving. All I got out of Henrik's fancy dinner was a shrimp!"

He opened the wine and poured himself a glass. "Cheers," he said, snagging another samosa as I devoured my meal.

⚓

I heard the little plane overhead sometime after midnight. When I first woke, I thought it was just Jay's snoring, but that really sounds more like a 747, not a small bush plane.

Wonder where he's going? I thought, half-asleep, flipping over on my side. And did he take her with him?

20

Jay was singing in the shower when I woke the next morning. Bellowing over the sound of the water, he was clearly in a great mood. That didn't last long, though. Felix brought bad news with the coffee.

He set the tray on the table before speaking. "There will be no game drive this morning, Miss. Everyone is asked to gather at breakfast at 8:00 for an announcement."

"Oh, I'm sorry. That's too bad. I was looking forward to it."

"What seems to be the problem, Felix?" Jay asked. "Is something wrong?"

Felix hesitated a moment before answering, and I had a feeling that something was indeed wrong. But if so, Felix wasn't sharing.

He was already backing out of the door. "I was told to ask everyone to come to the dining hall, Sir. That is all I can say."

"Okay, we'll be there. Thanks, Felix."

Jay waved goodbye and closed and locked the door before he climbed back into his bed.

"What do you think is the problem, Jay?"

"Who knows? Maybe he fed the drunk woman to the leopard. Canceling the game drive means extra time before breakfast, though. That's good. I'm finished in the shower, Sidney. Your turn. You probably have enough time for one of those long baths that you love so much. I'm going back to sleep."

He was right. I closed the bathroom door, turned on the taps, and poured in some bath oil. Soaking in the fragrant water, Jacuzzi running, I watched as the sky lightened, streaked with the first rays of the morning sun.

I could not see the riverbed through the glass wall, only the thick vegetation of the opposite bank. More importantly, anyone lurking in the riverbed wouldn't be able to see me either.

Two baboons appeared in the near branches, squabbling over a piece of fruit. Relaxing, I dismissed all thoughts of Henrik van der Brugge and his domestic problems.

⋈

Finally dressed and ready for the day, I grabbed a mug of coffee from Felix's carafe and joined Jay on our little back porch.

The morning mist had lifted with the dawn. The night sounds had given way to the raucous squawking of birds in a nearby tree and the chatter of monkeys. The sun was blazing in the east. The day would be a hot one, no jacket required.

Jay was sprawled in the hammock, holding his camera and methodically clicking back through its memory. Giggles from the hut next door let us know that Wendy and Tilda were also awake and out on their deck. We couldn't see them—and they couldn't see us, thanks to the clever way the huts had been angled when they were built—but we could certainly hear them.

"I'll bet those two giggle in their sleep," I said, sitting on the bench.

"They probably do, but they are really sweet, aren't they? I felt so bad for them when the monkeys ruined their camera."

"Are you going to send them some of your pictures?" I asked.

"Yeah. When we get back home. I told them I would."

Jay is a pretty good photographer. Me, not so much. Jay takes the best shots in the agency. We often use his on our website.

He turned off the camera and put the lens cap back in place. Then he spoke quietly. For once, he was serious. That, in itself, was a shocker. So was what followed.

He watched me intently as he spoke. "Sid, I hate to have to say this, because I know it will get you all stirred up." He stopped swinging, sat up and looked at me. "I'm not so sure it was monkeys that tore up Wendy and Tilda's hut."

I almost dropped my coffee mug. "What do you mean, Jay? It was monkeys. They said they saw them. Felix chased them out with the broom."

"I heard what they said. But I've decided there was a lot more to it than that. So, okay, the monkeys were in the hut. That's a fact. But maybe the camera was smashed and the memory card taken *before* the monkeys got in. In fact, maybe someone let the monkeys in to cover the fact that they had been there. Wendy and Tilda said they thought the hut was locked when they left and they are pretty careful about their stuff. I can't see those two leaving a door open, can you?"

"No, I can't. They seem so silly, but they are careful. That's true. I've noticed that."

He stood and walked toward me, speaking faster now, making a jury argument. I could tell he had given his theory a lot of thought. "The monkeys made a mess in the room, right? But the only thing missing was the memory card. That's odd, don't you think? What would monkeys want with a memory card? It's not shiny or anything. I don't think the monkeys took it, hon. I think someone else did."

"Who though? Not Felix. It wouldn't be Felix. I think he's totally trustworthy."

Jay sat next to me on the bench. "I do, too. No, not Felix. Not Winsome. I know they both have keys, but I'm sure there are other keys around too. It was someone else. Someone who broke in, took the memory card, smashed the camera, then left in a hurry—"

"Leaving the door open so the monkeys would get in, tear stuff up, and take the blame."

"Yes."

He stood up and stretched, carefully looping his camera back around his big neck by the strap. An eland, picking his way down the riverbed, saw him and bolted. The first strong rays of sun threw the overhanging bank below into shadow.

"Why?"

"Because somebody didn't like a picture Wendy took, that's why. That's what I think, anyway. That's all it can be. It wasn't your ordinary sneak thief. Nothing of value was taken. Memory cards are cheap."

What he said made perfect sense. There was clearly more to this incident than monkey mischief. "A real thief would have taken the whole camera, not just the memory card, and other stuff as well."

"Yes. And with her camera out of action, Wendy can't be snapping all those photos of everything and everybody. I think something is going on here, under the surface. Something *wrong*."

Jay went on, "I don't take anywhere near as many photos as Wendy, but I like to take random shots with my camera, too. So I was checking back through mine this morning to see if I might have caught anything unusual."

Confession time. "Jay, I know of at least one guy who would like to have her pictures erased."

He stopped pacing . "Who?"

"Well, I don't know his name, but ..." And I told him about seeing the man from the Nellie garden walking in the dry riverbed. I told him about Wendy taking the man's picture, and what his reaction had been.

"There," he said, with a told-you-so expression. "You

see? That's just what I mean. There may be a perfectly legitimate reason why the guy didn't like being photographed. Maybe he was having a bad hair day. Maybe he thinks photos steal his soul. Or maybe there's a real reason why he can't afford to be identified."

I leaned back, massaging my temples with my fingers. My headache was returning with all this. "Did you find anything in your camera memory?"

"No. But I'm not really sure what I'm looking for. Maybe you should click back through it to see if you can spot that guy you saw. I've never seen him, remember?

He took the camera from around his neck and handed it to me. "Another, thing, Sid," he said, sitting down beside me, "thinking about this today led me to consider what you said last night about this place and our host's income stream. Then I thought about Dennis, and again about the camera and the monkeys. That's when I decided that something funny might be going on, something strange. Maybe I'm being overly suspicious. Maybe it's nothing, just a feeling. But I think we need to keep our heads up from now on, babe, and discuss anything odd that we notice. Not with the others. Just us. There's no need to freak out about it. Don't mention it, don't talk it up. Just be observant and careful until this tour is over. That's all I'm saying."

I watched his eyes, usually so merry and now so somber and serious that it ramped up my own uneasiness. "I have to tell you, it freaks me out to hear you say that, Jay. I'm usually the suspicious one, not you. If you're worried, it's huge."

Jay ran his fingers through his hair, making it stick up all over. Another bad sign. He does that when he's upset. "I wouldn't call it *worried*, exactly," he said. "More like cautious. I'm just saying, Sidney, don't let all this funny stuff or what I think spoil your trip. Just keep your eyes and ears open. That's all. And, more importantly, your mouth shut. This whole safari operation may be a big fake. This place could be an elaborate front for something else, at the very least, a money-laundering scheme."

"Jay, do you know something you're not telling me? Don't keep secrets."

He squeezed my hand. "No, babe. No secrets. At this point it's just a feeling I have. I have absolutely no hard evidence and I'm not sure I want to find any. Not my job. Not *our* job. We're only here for a few more days; then it's out of the bush and back to Cape Town and civilization."

"True," I said. "But don't you think we need to alert Silverstein to check this deal out further before we go bringing any High Steppers in here? Remember what he said, 'No slipups.' And the part about holding us personally responsible? I'm pretty sure that if we end up with another mess on our hands, we'll be out of a job."

Jay ran his hands through his hair again before he answered. It looked as if it had been electrified. I knew he was thinking about how dire his financial situation would be if he was unemployed. "You bet we should," he said. "We should absolutely tell Silverstein, and time is short. He'll be signing a contract and printing brochures soon, if he hasn't already. We need to get the word to him if we can, as soon as we can, though that may not be possible until we return to Cape Town. We'll tell him to take a long look before he signs anything with these people. He doesn't have to cancel his safari plans. There are lots of other good lodges he can use. I just think it might be better if he steers clear of this one."

I shook my head. "I don't think we'll be able to call New York for a few days, Jay. It will be tough to connect with Silverstein from here. We're 'isolated from the cares of the world,' remember?"

"Yeah, but not really. We can't be. Van der Brugge doesn't seem to have any problems communicating. You might have to sneak back into his house and make a phone call."

"What?"

He raised his hands in protest. "Just kidding, just kidding. Don't have a hissy. I'll figure something out. There's the breakfast bell. Let's go. Lock that door up tight, babe, and check it. We don't want any *monkeys* in here."

⧗

When we started down the steps, I saw that the path outside Hut No. 1 had been neatly swept with a twig broom, as it was every morning. Even so, fresh animal tracks had already marked the sandy soil.

A pair of Thompson's gazelles watched us from the small meadow as we reached the main path. They broke into a run, leaping as they disappeared into the brush.

"*Buon giorno,*" Fernando said, stepping out of his hut as we passed. "It is a beautiful morning, eh? I am hungry for my breakfast. I think sleeping in fresh air causes such hunger. I must stop eating like this or I will get very, very fat, like an opera singer."

Admiring his spare, muscular frame, outlined through his tight T-shirt, I thought there was little chance of that. My cousin Earline would say his body was "mighty fine." *And Earline*, I thought, *would be correct.*

He joined us on the path as we marched on toward breakfast.

A sudden movement caught my eye. I looked back toward Fernando's hut just in time to see Winsome slip away from his door, carrying her twig broom. She looked a bit furtive and disheveled as she disappeared into the thicket behind the hut.

I wondered what she was doing, and where she had spent the night.

George joined us from the path his hut shared with Fernando's. We all continued on in that fresh morning air, looking forward to the good meal that awaited us in the huge thatched lodge.

We were not disappointed. The breakfast was lavish, beginning with ripe mango, melon, and pineapple, followed by omelets, crepes, and big baskets of muffins and toast.

"Good morning, ladies and gentlemen," David trilled, tapping on his glass with a spoon. "I hope you weren't too disappointed with the cancellation of our morning game drive, because we have a *marvelous* treat in store for us today. Mr. van der Brugge *himself* will be here *soon* to announce it. Enjoy your breakfast, my dears. I shall not spoil the surprise, not even with the *tiniest* hint, but I can assure you that we may all look forward to his announcement with *great anticipation*."

"What do y'all think it is?" asked Connie, buttering another scone. "I hope it's something different. I'm getting tired of all these animals. I mean, they were awesome at first, but I'm ready to move on."

"Me, too," said Chase. "I'm ready for something new."

Rick looked at Chase like he wanted to smack him. "Chase," he said, "the only animals you've even glimpsed on this entire trip are the ones at the waterhole by the swimming pool. You haven't been out on either of the game drives so far. Before we signed up you promised you would go on at least one."

Chase shrugged. "Well, I was going to go on that one today, Rich, but they called it off. That's not my fault, obviously. I was all ready."

Chase must have been telling the truth, for the magnificent and expensive safari clothes he was wearing put Jay's in the shade. Sadly, that fact was not lost on Jay.

"I think this whole operation is a big waste," Mabel screeched from the next table. "Useless. I don't believe in squandering valuable time like this, lolling around a pool with no purpose. I believe in action. True ecotourism. There's work that should be done here. Problems that need to be ferreted out and corrected. My people would never come to a place like this. Never."

"Thank God for that," Jay muttered. "I expect the Leopard Dance folks will be relieved to hear that."

"Yeah," said Connie. "I mean, why did she want to come on this fam with all of us in the first place? This whole deal was described in the brochure and on the website. Honestly. Is she really a travel agent? I wish I'd brought my mink along on the trip to show her. That would really send her over the edge."

"Your mink? A real fur coat? Do you really have a fur coat?" Chase asked.

"You bet your sweet ass, I do," she said, sitting a little straighter. "Full-length. My first husband bought it for me after I caught him in the backseat of his Cadillac with a cocktail waitress. I didn't stay married to him long after that, just long enough to get the mink and stock up on the latest makeup. Then it was bye-bye, Bubba."

"You said your first husband," Rich said. "How many husbands have you had?"

"Three," Fernando said.

"None of them were worth a damn," said Connie. "I told y'all I'm on the lookout for a new one. Maybe I'll get lucky this time."

She gave Fernando a smoldering look and a wink and stuck out her chest. Everyone laughed.

※

"May I have your attention, please?"

Henrik van der Brugge had entered the room and stood in front of the fire pit, clapping his hands for attention. He looked as handsome as ever and none the worse for wear after the violent nocturnal arrival of his bride, or ex-bride, whichever she was.

I wondered what had become of her. Since he was standing before us, he had clearly not been a passenger in the little airplane I had heard leaving in the night. Her car was certainly not drivable, so maybe she had left in the plane. I hoped she had. I didn't want any more quality time with that nutty woman.

Van der Brugge's eyes took in the whole room as he began to speak, although he never looked directly at me.

"Good morning, ladies and gentlemen. It is a beautiful morning here at Leopard Dance, yes? Today, I have a surprise for you. Unfortunately, Willem tells me that we must shut off the water here in camp after breakfast for about twelve hours, for some routine maintenance to the pumps. So, I am announcing a change in plans, a slight departure from our normal routine. It is my gift to you, a special treat."

Tilda and Wendy clapped and started whispering and giggling to each other, speculating on what the surprise might be.

Van der Brugge paused until they settled down.

"Please, continue to enjoy your breakfast," he smiled. "Take your time, and when you have finished, I would ask that you return to your rooms. There, on your beds, you will find a small cloth bag. In it, you may pack whatever you need for one night and bring it along with you to the reception pavilion by ten o'clock. Only that bag, the bag I have provided, please. Nothing else. At ten, you will board the usual vehicles. You will not be returning to the lodge until tomorrow morning. We are going camping."

Hands shot up with questions. Wendy and Tilda, Mabel, Chase, and Rose each wanted to ask something; everyone was excited and curious. But van der Brugge just smiled even more and headed for the door, saying over his shoulder, "Our destination is a surprise. Please be prompt. We leave at ten."

After his exit, we bombarded David with questions, but he claimed to know nothing about the plans, not even our destination.

"I say, this is *thrilling*, what? A *splendid surprise* for me, too. Mr. van der Brugge called me aside just before the breakfast bell and told me he had something special in store for us. Quite *exciting*, isn't it? No, I don't know where we are going. He didn't say. That is all part of the excitement, not knowing where one is going. Now hurry along, my dears, and pack your things. Remember now, only the little bags on your beds. Nothing else will be allowed."

21

Choosing what to pack for the overnight was tough for Jay. Not much fit into the small, native-print cotton tote bag he found on his bed. Sleepwear, a change of underwear, a fresh shirt, and basic toiletries quickly filled it. He's a big guy, and his clothes are big, too. Everything Jay owns—clothing and personal care items—takes up more room than mine. Plus, I don't plan my clothes in ensembles.

"I could sleep commando and have room for my D&G slacks, Sidney. Would that be okay with you?"

"No. It would not. You don't need fresh pants tomorrow, Jay. We'll only be gone for one night. Just take a clean shirt and underwear and wear the same pants you have on now tomorrow. That's what I'm doing."

His face fell. "Then it won't match. I had my outfits all worked out. This is going to goof it all up."

I extended my hand. "Give me the pants, Jay. I have a little room left in my bag. I think I can cram them in with my stuff."

After all these years of traveling, I can totally pack a bag for a trip. I plan my outfits with the itinerary, laying them all out on the bed, taking the weather predictions into consideration. I pack my bag in layers, placing my underwear, sleepwear and swimsuits in zip-top plastic bags on the bottom. I put shoes and belts around the edges, roll up everything else, and jam it in as tight as I can. Folded jackets, dresses, and dressy pants go on top.

A tight bag, with clothes carefully folded or rolled,

prevents wrinkles. That seems crazy, but it's true. When things are loosely packed, they move around in the bag and end up really rumpled. I always add a sheet of copy paper, printed with my name, cellphone number, and address, into the top inside pocket in case the bag goes astray with the tags torn off. You wouldn't believe the stuff I can cram into a bag. My bag is like a magic hat.

Jay knows how to do that, too, but has a harder time because his stuff is so enormous, and because he just can't stand breaking up his carefully coordinated outfits. I guess that would be hard for me, too, if I spent all my paycheck and then some on expensive clothes and fashion magazines.

"Don't wad them all up. Those pants are new, and they're really nice."

Please.

I took out all my stuff and started over, repacking the little cotton bag. To accommodate Jay's long pants, I switched the long-sleeved white cotton shirt I had planned to pack for a skimpier, thin cotton knit in smoky gray. Jay's pants, carefully folded, went on top.

The big baby's mood was a lot sunnier once he realized that he would still be able to bring the pants he needed to complete his look.

"I'm glad you switched shirts," he said. "I like that gray shirt on you, Sidney. It's almost the exact color of your eyes."

I gave him a long look. "You are just saying that because I had to ditch my other shirt to make room for your pants. The last time I wore the gray one you said I looked like a burglar."

"Well, you do, because you insist on wearing it with those black jeans."

"Whatever."

Jay may not have had room enough for his pants, but he somehow managed to force a bottle of wine and a corkscrew down into his bag.

I wasn't going to let him get away with that. "I thought you were worried about wrinkles and space," I said. "Why are you taking that bottle in your bag? They'll surely have wine wherever we're going."

"Well, we don't know that, do we? So I'm coming prepared."

I zipped up my bag. "Well, that's good, I guess. You know, I think this little mystery outing might really be fun, although I question van de Brugge's motives in offering it. Do you think he's trying to distract us with this outing so we'll stop thinking of the bad things that have happened in the camp? That would make sense. After all, he invited us here to boost his business. He's trying to emphasize the positives in the safari experience at his lodge, and death by leopard is about the biggest negative I can imagine."

"Yeah, or he just wants to get us away from the lodge tonight for his own reasons."

"Like what? What reasons? Why do you think he planned this overnight away from camp, Jay? Arranging all this has to be a lot more trouble and expense for him than to just let everything rock on as planned."

"Exactly," Jay said, "and when I try to think of why he might be doing this, none of the answers that come to mind seem to stem from kindheartedness or generosity. There's the bell. Move it, babe. Let's go find out where your boyfriend is taking us."

I didn't answer that. My grandmother says that if you can't say something nice, you shouldn't say anything at all.

22

"Crocodiles," said George, peering anxiously through his big red glasses down into the river as we wound our way slowly along its edge. "I do *not* do crocodiles."

There were certainly lots of them.

Scores of crocodiles lay bunched together, sunning themselves on a sandbar at the edge of the river. Huge, fat crocodiles.

"Look how big they are," Connie said. "They look like they're sleeping. They must have just eaten. Wonder what they ate?"

"Wonder *who* they ate," George muttered.

George had been nervous and fidgety all morning. The move from camp had clearly taken him way out of his comfort zone.

After Dennis' tragic demise, George finally had his hut all to himself. He was gleeful about it and happy to tell anyone who would listen that his life was much better now that Dennis was gone. Jay declared that any remorse George had exhibited over Dennis' passing was completely fake. I agreed. The only remorseful words I could recall George speaking was when he said he was sorry that Dennis was eaten.

George had settled comfortably into the rhythm of life at the safari lodge, almost as if he had always lived there. He loved his luxurious little hut, and the idea of an overnight expedition did not please him one bit. He did not like being uprooted, so he was griping about every little thing.

Jay said the campout was all Connie's fault. "They

probably overheard you, Peaches, complaining with Chase about being bored. You made them think we needed some excitement."

Jay had renamed Connie "Peaches" because she had let it slip over cocktails that she was once chosen Peach Queen in her home state of Georgia. Jay loved the nickname. "Peaches" she would be to Jay forevermore.

"How could they know what we said?" Connie retorted. "We only said it to you all. Not even David was there."

"Eyes and ears are everywhere at this lodge," Jay continued, "and they all report back to the boss. They want us to be happy so we'll go back home and recommend a lot of bookings. I say that you, Peaches, and Chase are the main cause of the big move. I don't mind, though. Now that I've thought it over, I've decided it might be fun."

He looked over at George, who was slumped down in his seat, wearing sunglasses, his hat pulled down low over his face. He was pouting like a baby because he didn't get his way. His objections had been ignored.

"Get over it, George," Jay said. "This little trip is not optional. You have to go, so you might as well stop whining and get with the program."

I had to agree. Plus, the change of scene would allow us an opportunity to see the extreme Northern part of Kruger, which had not been on our original itinerary. Jay had pestered Vincent as we loaded until he told him we were headed north, through Kruger, to a tented camp near the border of South Africa. I was excited about the unexpected bonus and I knew Jay was, too, whether he admitted it or not.

The Kruger National Park is the oldest game park in South Africa. Named for South Africa's first president Paul Kruger, it is bordered on the north by the Limpopo River and Zimbabwe, on the east by Mozambique, and on the south by the Crocodile River. Long and narrow, it is the largest of the game reserves—220 miles from north to south and 38 miles wide.

Leopard Dance is in a private reserve on the western border of Kruger, about midway, so it took a drive of over a hundred miles that morning to reach the tented camp on the south banks of the Limpopo.

We drove north through Kruger and headed for the river, enjoying the abundant wildlife along the way. Kruger contains all of the Big Five: lion, leopard, elephant, rhino, and Cape buffalo. It is a big deal in African safaris to spot all of the Big Five in a single trip. In that one morning drive, we saw one pride of lions, several large herds of Cape buffalo, elephants, and lots of different species of antelope, such as eland, roan, sable and grysbok.

Vincent paused now and then in our journey to allow viewing and photographing of the wildlife. On one such stop he pointed out a large bird that David had identified for us in his slide presentation on the morning after our arrival in Cape Town.

Jay stood up in the Rover and cracked the whole group up by pointing dramatically at the bird and screaming out, "By Jove, George, it's a Corey bustard!"

Jay was far more relaxed that day than he'd been ever since leaving Cape Town. He didn't even flinch as we neared a small pride of blood-streaked lions, sleeping in the sun after devouring an antelope, the remains of which lay nearby.

"Are you feeling better about all this, Jay?" I asked quietly. "You seem to be actually enjoying the animals."

"Yes. I am, Sidney. Somehow I no longer feel as if we are meals on wheels."

The terrain changed as we moved north, becoming more arid as we wove our way through mahogany, ebony, fever, and wild fig trees. Leaving the main road through Kruger on its western edge, we passed through the boundary gate. The last part of our long drive was on a red sand road among a wilderness of mopane trees—a tall, shrub-like tree with butterfly shaped leaves.

Vincent braked the Rover, made a sharp left around an ancient baobab tree, then a right, and finally slowed as he turned into a lane marked with a carved wooden sign that said, "Pearl Moon Tented Camp." At the end of the road we could see a group of large, white platform tents that had been erected along the south bank of the river in a grove of fever trees. The other vehicles pulled into the lane behind us. Vincent was driving slowly, the wheels barely turning, to reduce our dust near the camp.

"That's where I'm sleeping? In a flimsy canvas tent next to a nest of crocodiles?" George said. "No way."

"Yes," said Vincent, "We'll unload here. When we stop, please bring your bags and follow Anthony to the dining tent. Ingwe is there, waiting to greet us with refreshments."

For once, Mabel was silent. She seemed preoccupied and had spoken only a word or two since leaving Leopard Dance. I wondered what she was thinking.

I was warming to Mabel. I still didn't like her much but I thought my first impression of her might have been wrong. She could certainly be abrasive and harsh, but I did not join Jay and George in their intense dislike of her. I was getting used to her rough way of speaking and was beginning to realize that behind her annoying exterior, she might actually be a decent person.

She was odd. No doubt about that. But it seemed to me that Mabel might be good at heart after all, even if her manner of speaking was brash and annoying. Mabel did not have much use for humans, but her advocacy for animals was admirable.

I totally agreed with her about the rhinos. I shared her conviction that the dreadful slaughter of the innocent beasts must be stopped before they all disappeared forever from the Earth.

Mabel had been seated next to me for the drive, just behind Jay and George and in front of Connie and Chase.

Rich had chosen to ride in one of the other vehicles, and Mabel had taken his spot. Rich and Chase weren't speaking to each other. They were apparently having one of their frequent spats. Those happened often, but usually did not last long. I expected them to make up before lunch.

Our long impromptu journey took us from Leopard Dance all the way to the banks of Kipling's "great, grey-green, greasy Limpopo River."

"Why have we come all this way?" Mabel finally demanded of Vincent, breaking her silence. "There's something fishy about all this. Why were we hustled away so suddenly from our lodge? What are we doing in this place?"

"I do not know, Madam. Something about the water pumps," Vincent replied. "Mr. van der Brugge does not discuss his plans with us or give us his reasons. We are paid to follow his orders. We drive where he tells us, when he tells us, that's all. You must ask him. He is there, waiting."

"Does he own this place, too?" Chase asked.

Chase always wanted to know who owned what. We had learned early on that he was the type of guy who likes to try to cozy up to people he considers rich or important.

"Partially," Vincent said. "This tented camp belongs to Spieël Provisioners, a company he owns in partnership with one of his friends and business associates, Mr. Hsu. Spieël actually owns Leopard Dance, too. Willem is also a partner, but a very small one. Mr. van der Brugge owns the majority."

"Hsu?" Chase asked. "That doesn't sound like a South African."

"Mr. Hsu is not native," said Vincent. "I believe he is Chinese. He lives in Hong Kong."

Vincent parked underneath a huge baobab tree, its branches providing welcome shade. The day was heating up. Velvet monkeys screeched and scolded us from the branches above. Jay helped me down from the Rover, handing me my little bag.

"I hate to admit Mabel is right about anything, Sidney, but she has a point," he murmured as we followed the others up the path toward the camp. "As she said, we really have come a long way on what seems to be our host's whim. That's what I thought originally and now I really believe it. This sudden little jaunt seems strange to me, too."

"Yes," I whispered back, "but as long as we're here, Jay, we might as well enjoy it. I'm glad to get a chance to stay in a tented camp. I've heard of them, but I've never seen one. We'd never in a million years be bringing High Steppers here. It's not on the negotiated itinerary and Silverstein is not about to spring for anything extra."

Jay nodded. "True. So true. He'd pass out if he knew we were even here, wasting valuable time on a side trip that Itchy won't be selling. There's no way to call him from here, either, about the contract. That will just have to wait."

23

As we neared the largest of the tents, I spotted Henrik van der Brugge standing at the entrance, talking with Willem. It was the first time I had seen him since my hasty retreat from our disaster of a dinner party. I wondered what he would say, or if he would pretend it had never happened.

As usual, he looked handsome in tan safari clothing and tall, polished boots. On his broad shoulders, the safari clothes looked absolutely right. On Jay and Chase, they looked like a costume.

The platform of the largest tent was elevated, encircled on all sides by a deck with a bamboo railing and reached by a set of wooden steps. Folding canvas lounge chairs and small tables had been placed at intervals around the deck, allowing for leisurely comfort within view of the river. A workman was stretching a white rope hammock between two poles in one corner. Another hammock, in the opposite corner, was already in place.

Two sides of the canvas walls had been rolled up and tied, allowing the breeze to pass through. The wind caused the branches of the great trees flanking the tent to sway gently.

As we started up the steps, Willem went back inside and van der Brugge began greeting the first of the group. Mabel pounced on him with her questions. He pulled her aside, down a partitioned hallway, away from the entrance, to answer them.

"She's giving him hell," Connie laughed. "Look at her pointing that bony finger in his face. She jumped on him like a duck on a June bug."

150

Willem had walked away from van der Brugge and Mabel and resumed directing the arrangement of a buffet lunch. Men from the camp's kitchen staff set out large serving platters filled with salads, meats, and vegetables on a long rectangular table. A round, skirted table nearby was loaded with desserts.

The main buffet table was covered with a broad white cloth and centered with a lavish arrangement of fruit and flowers. Just to the left of it, a side table held stacks of folded linen napkins, white china plates, and trays of silverware.

It looked elegant and glamorous. Even after our big breakfast, everyone was ready to eat, drink, and relax.

Rebecca was welcoming guests near the entrance where van der Brugge had been standing before Mabel jumped him. She offered tall drinks from a nearby tray stand. I took one, glad to have it after the long, hot ride.

"They really do this up right, don't they?" said Chase.

I had to agree. It was perfect, reminding me of scene in a movie.

I knew Jay thought so, too. He was in his element. I could see his imagination at work, as he pictured himself starring in a classic scene from the movie *Elephant Walk.*

That old film was one of several we had rented before coming to Africa. Jay and I always do that before big trips— rent movies and read books about the country we plan to visit. If you can find the time in the rush of packing and last-minute chores, it really enhances a trip. It puts you in the mood for the trip you are about to take and whets your appetite for the places you are soon to see.

Elephant Walk, one of the films we watched, is one of Jay's all-time favorites. It is actually set in old Ceylon, rather than Africa, but it is just the sort of sweeping epic that Jay loves. Even with that setting, Jay insisted that we could include it on our list along with *Out of Africa* because elephants are important in the film. The plot centers on a proud man who willfully builds a splendid mansion directly across the path of an ancient elephant trail, forcing the huge beasts to alter their customary path.

As Jay strolled around the handsome tented pavilion in his safari suit, I could see him getting into character in his mind. I could tell from the way he stood, drink in hand, overlooking the river. In his imagination, Jay *was* Montgomery Cliff, the leading actor from the old film.

In my imagination, the role of the proud, defiant master would be far better suited to Henrik van de Brugge. There was a sense of command about him, in the way he stood, in the way he walked. Not arrogance exactly, just the assurance of a man who knew exactly what he wanted from life. Whatever that was, watching him, I was sure he would achieve it, if he hadn't already. He seemed fully in control of his surroundings.

I expect the reason I was attracted to him in the first place was that he reminded me a bit of another commanding man, one from whom I had recently parted. The thought of that man cast a shadow over my day. I still wasn't sure that I had made the right decision in suspending our relationship. My friend Brooke's words rang in my memory, "Think carefully, Sidney. Be sure you know what you are doing. He may not wait for you to come back to him."

I remembered the grave look in her blue eyes, usually so merry, when she said it.

Ting-ting-ting-ting.

The sound of David tapping on a glass for attention roused me from my reverie.

"Attention, please. Attention, ladies and gentlemen. An *absolute feast* has been prepared for us. Please come."

The lunch line was forming, with David and Tilda and Wendy in the lead, as always, followed by Mabel. Connie and Rose had gone to the ladies' room.

Van der Brugge, having escaped Mabel's tirade, had

stepped to one side of the buffet table where he stood talking quietly with Willem.

Jay, George, Chase, and Rich were at the bar on their second round of drinks. They didn't look as if they would be lining up for the buffet anytime soon. As predicted, Chase and Rich had made up.

"Come, *cara mia*," Fernando said, interrupting my thoughts. "Let's get our plates and take them out on the deck so we can see the river. It is a beautiful day. We may spot something interesting."

It may have been childish of me, but I was glad to lunch with handsome Fernando while Henrik van der Brugge watched. I still had not spoken with him because Mabel pounced before I got a chance.

The line began to move, and Fernando and I joined it, filling our plates with fruit, baked chicken with a delicate lemon sauce, and rice pilaf. I also took a large serving of okra, onions, and tomato, stewed together with basil.

Fernando peered at my plate. "What is that vegetable, Sidney? I've never seen it before."

"It's okra, Fernando. Try some, I think you'll enjoy it. It's an African vegetable that grows on tall, stalky plants. We also grow it in my home state of Mississippi. Okra originated in Africa. Where I'm from, in the South, okra is a staple. As a child I didn't like it, but I love it now. My mother serves it many ways—by itself, in a gumbo, and of course, fried. It really is delicious."

He gave me a puzzled look. "Gumbo?"

"A sort of soup, made with a dark roux, served with rice. Gumbo almost always contains okra and usually shrimp and crabmeat."

We took our plates and drinks to the far corner of the deck. Fernando pulled a small table and two chairs a bit away from the others and out of the sun, into the deep shade. He had chosen a good spot. Though we could see all that went on in the tent as well as a full view of the river, we were out of the way. Our chairs were set back from the others.

Lunching with Fernando on the open-air porch near the great river was delightful. Laughing at amusing tales of his life as an international airline rep caused the shadow of my earlier thoughts to fade into the background. Intent on his stories, I was barely aware that most of the others had finished lunch and moved back inside, out of the sun and heat.

The temperature had risen steadily along with the sun, which now blazed overhead. In the shelter of the great fever trees, with the breeze blowing, our table was cool and pleasant despite the temperature.

Everything seemed to have slowed in the heat. No animals were visible just then in that section of the river, only some wading birds. Birds were everywhere, standing in the shallows, flying overhead, calling from the branches of the trees.

"It's hard to believe that a scene so tranquil can become violent so quickly," Fernando said, as we finished our meal. He placed his napkin on the table and moved his chair closer to mine, out of a patch of sunlight.

"Violent, really? Here? It seems so serene."

"I do not know about this exact spot, but yes, violence can erupt at any time anywhere along this border. The Limpopo is the boundary, the border, between South Africa and Zimbabwe. Zimbabwe, which was formerly known as Southern Rhodesia, is there." He pointed. "See?" he said. "That's Zimbabwe, just across the river."

As if to disprove his disturbing words of potential violence, two Oryx appeared on the opposite bank. The pair moved gracefully on delicate-looking legs toward the water's edge. They bent their white-masked heads, crowned with long, straight horns, for a drink. It was hard to imagine a more peaceful scene.

Just as their lips touched the water, a crocodile, which

had been lying concealed nearby in the reeds, lunged for them. One Oryx escaped in a flash, moving too quickly for the monster. He bolted away from what would have been certain death.

The other was not so lucky. Thrashing in the shallows, he struggled in vain to pull his leg from the croc's powerful jaws. The ancient beast pulled his prize into deeper water and began his death roll. We watched in horrified fascination until the crocodile and his catch sank beneath the surface and the roiling water became still again.

"It is as I said. You see?" Fernando smiled, "Danger is everywhere here, *tesoro*. Death can come swiftly, without warning."

I looked into his smiling eyes, wondering what he was really saying. "Are you just speaking of the animals, Fernando, or of men, too?"

"Well, they are all animals, aren't they, the violent ones? This is a land of great poverty and great riches, Sidney. Gold, diamonds, the extremely profitable horns and tusks of animals ... it is all here for the taking. Only the law and the efforts of a few good men stand in the way. Greed is a powerful force. The veneer of civilization becomes very thin when so much treasure is at stake."

A waiter approached with a tray, collecting plates, followed by another passing desserts, and yet another with cups of coffee. We refused dessert, but gladly accepted the coffee.

"Anything bad here is much worse across the river in Zimbabwe," he continued. "Their economy is in shambles. In 2009, they even had to abandon their currency. They use the U.S. dollar now."

Settling back in the chair with his mug of coffee, Fernando's somber mood changed as he began telling me another string of amusing tales, this time of his prior African adventures. His stories were light and funny, his serious words of warning seemingly forgotten.

But they were still there, beneath the laughter, somewhere in the shadows of his dark eyes. The warning remained, underneath the surface like the crocodile, lurking in the "grey-green waters of the Limpopo."

24

"Ladies and gentlemen," David called, clapping his hands, from the center of the pavilion, "gather round, please, gather round. That was a *splendid* lunch, wasn't it? A *magnificent repast!* Please join me in thanking our *gracious* host, Mr. van der Brugge, for bringing us to this *spectacular* place and giving us this *unexpected treat.*"

He swiveled his head, looking for our gracious host, but van der Brugge was gone.

Miffed that Henrik was not there to receive his flowery compliments, David plunged instead into a torrent of words, describing the options available to us for the afternoon and evening. What it basically boiled down to—when you winnowed out all the puff—was an optional afternoon game walk, cocktails, then dinner with entertainment by a local folkloric group performing traditional songs and dances.

"This special treat will be an *unexpected delight.* Please feel free to join in the singing and dancing at this *most unusual* entertainment."

"Crass commercial exploitation, that's all it is," was Mabel's acid comment. For once, however, she didn't follow up her complaint with an impassioned speech. Mabel was definitely off her game.

David gave her a hard look, which she ignored. Then he introduced Rebecca, who gave housekeeping details and issued sleeping assignments, along with cautions about keeping our tents zipped shut when leaving them. She warned everyone not to venture out alone anywhere, particularly near the river.

"Don't you worry one minute about that, sister," Connie said. "I ain't going *nowhere* near that river!"

Wendy and Tilda were whispering and giggling to each other as usual, but Mabel was still strangely silent. Again, I wondered what was going on with her and resolved to ask at first opportunity.

"The game walk will begin from this place at four o'clock p.m.," Rebecca said. "Please be on time or you will be left behind. We must finish our walk before sunset. Remember to bring your cameras and binoculars."

I hung around the deck until everyone headed to their tents. Then, instead of going to my tent, I found Mabel's.

#

"Yes? What is it?"

Mabel poked her head out of the tent opening, clearly annoyed at being disturbed.

"Hi, Mabel. I'm sorry to bother you, but I wondered if you could spare a few moments to talk with me in private. I think it might be important."

She looked to be on the verge of telling me to go away, but then she must have changed her mind. Unzipping the opening all the way, she motioned impatiently for me to enter.

"What's on your mind, Sidney? Make it quick, I want to take a nap. I didn't sleep much last night."

"Mabel, I think we started off on the wrong foot, and I just wanted to say that I am in total agreement with you about the poaching of the rhino and elephants."

"That's nice," she snapped. "But that's not why you are here. You could say that anytime, in front of anyone."

"Yes, you're right. I could."

"Well then, what is it? What did you come to tell me?"

"Mabel, Jay and I agree that there's something strange

about this particular camp. We think there might be things going on here behind the scenes that escape the notice of the regular visitor. Today, I noticed that you have been really quiet and distracted, and I wondered if you shared some of our misgivings about this operation. I even thought you might have noticed something or discovered information that we need to know. Jay and I are responsible to our agency for checking this tour out for our clients. We certainly don't want to recommend anything that might be illegal or even dangerous for them."

She gave me a searching stare, squinting those beady eyes at me. It made her look meaner and more wrinkled than ever. She was sizing me up, wondering if she could trust me.

Finally, she spoke. "Yes, Sidney, there is definitely something wrong here. I realized as soon as I got to this game lodge. I have a lot of experience in these matters. Before I retired and became a travel agent I used to work for the government. There is something going on here behind the scenes. I'm not ready yet to speak openly about it, but when I have one or two more facts nailed down I will. I'll shout it to the heavens. I'll tell the world. But I'm not quite ready. I am still finding things out. That's why I'm so tired. I was up most of the night."

"What is it? Will you tell me what you think is happening?"

"Like I said, Sidney, I'm still gathering information. When I have it all sorted out I'll be happy to tell you and everyone else. I'm very close to finding out everything I need to know. Another piece of the puzzle fell into place today. That's all I'll say for now. But I wouldn't plan to send any clients here if I were you. This operation may look beautiful to the casual observer, but underneath, it's rotten."

"I could help you—"

"No, you can't," she said, cutting me off in her rude way, "I don't need your help. I don't want your help. Actually, you've already helped me more than you know. If I need your assistance, I'll ask for it. Now please leave. I have to sleep."

With that, she clamped her mouth into the usual thin line, hustled me out of her tent, and zipped it shut.

♓

On the way to my tent, I thought over Mabel's words. She obviously shared our misgivings about Henrik van der Brugge's safari operation, and was, by her own account, hard at work investigating it.

I felt a great relief. Our misgivings were clearly not just the products of overactive imaginations. It bothers me more than I want to admit that trouble seems to follow me around on trips. Mean old Diana says I attract trouble, as if that were somehow possible. Jay teases me and calls me "MM" for "murder magnet." Even my friend Roz says I shouldn't leave New York without a gun and a rabbit's foot. It's bad enough that all this bad stuff seems to happen on my trips. It would be even worse if I started imagining trouble where none exists.

So my relief after talking with Mabel was twofold. First, my suspicions were confirmed. That was comforting in an odd way. And secondly, Mabel's dedication to her mission meant Jay and I weren't going to have to snoop after all. We could leave it all up to Mabel. I sure didn't want to get involved in any trouble if I could avoid it. Diana had given me strict instructions to steer clear of "unsavory situations." There *was* something odd going on for sure, but it looked as if I wasn't going to have to run point on this one.

Stop worrying, I told myself. *Punt! Can the curiosity and leave it all up to Mabel.*

The birds were singing overhead as I neared my tent, and the first of the spring flowers were popping out along the path. I resolved to stop worrying.

It was a beautiful day in a beautiful setting that was far removed from the concrete streets of my adopted home, New York, the city I love. I was lucky to be there and knew I might never have the chance again, so I made up my mind to shelve some of my misgivings about the camp operations and Dennis' strange demise, relax, be happy, and enjoy the safari while it lasted. That should please both Jay and Diana. But Mr. Silverstein was not going to be happy. If what we suspected proved to be true, no High Steppers would be coming to Leopard Dance. We wouldn't be recommending it.

Diana would just have to find him another safari lodge.

⟨⟩

Once again, Jay and I were assigned to share accommodations. This time he wasn't griping about it. I thought he was glad to have a roommate because we would be sleeping in tents without true walls or doors. He had calmed down about the animals at Leopard Dance, but here, in a new environment, his fears were returning. As soon as we entered our tent I learned that my guess was correct.

"A zipper," he ranted. "A zipper! That's all that will be keeping God knows who or what out of our tent tonight, Sidney. I'm not going to sleep a wink. *A zipper.* I ask you again, what on earth are we doing here? I wish I were back in camp, in good old Hut No. 1."

I was sprawled in a rattan camp chair under the slow-moving blades of an old-fashioned ceiling fan and sipping a lemonade in a tall, frosted glass.

"I think it's exciting, Jay. I love camping out, but camping for me is usually in a tiny dome tent with a Coleman lantern, not anything like this."

"Well, this is pretty posh, but I wish we were back at Leopard Dance. It felt a lot safer than this does, no matter how fancy it is."

The white canvas tent was huge, with a gleaming wooden floor and mahogany and rattan furniture. Twin four-poster beds, draped in white mosquito netting, were in the center of the room. There was a small ensuite toilet and shower. Really glamorous. I knew that once Jay conquered his fears, *if* he conquered his fears, he would love it.

"Jay, don't get all spooked about the animals again. You sound just like George. Relax. We have a little time before the game walk."

"*You* have a little time," he said, hooking the netting back up and stretching out on his bed. "*I* have lots of time, because I'm not going."

"What? Why not? You know the guards will be with us for the entire walk. It's safe. They are armed."

He waved his fingers at me. "Go! Bu-bye. Run along, Nature Girl. While you have fun, frolicking in the jungle, I'm going to the bar. I'll see you when you get back. *If* you get back. If not, I'll send a nice bouquet to your memorial service."

♓

I thought about Jay's funeral flowers two hours later when a monster elephant angrily trumpeted not fifty feet in front of me.

"Please be very still and quiet," Jerome whispered. "We are so close to him that he may charge if we anger him."

Everyone froze, even Wendy and Tilda. Their round blue eyes were huge.

With Jerome, our local game spotter, in the lead, we had walked west along a grassy track out of the tented camp. We followed Jerome and a local guide named Simon. Vincent brought up the rear with his big rifle.

The path started near the river, wound through the brush, then came alongside the river again. David, Mabel,

Rose, Tilda and Wendy, Rich, Fernando and even George had chosen to join the excursion. Chase, Connie, and Jay stayed at the bar. Just before we left, I had tried one last time to get Jay to go with us, but he still refused.

I was really surprised that George actually showed up at the meeting point. I'd have bet a week's pay that he would have been too frightened to go. The fact that even George was willing to do the nature walk should have changed Jay's mind, but it hadn't.

"I don't care if George is going," he insisted, "or anybody else. It makes no difference. I'm staying right here, and that's final."

Willem, placing a bowl of snacks on the bar, overheard what Jay said and shook his head. His sly blue eyes crinkled with laughter. Eventually I gave up on Jay and joined the group on the steps.

The first part of the walk was uneventful. It was peaceful, really, with the calls of the birds and chatter of monkeys. I was happy. Walking in the sunshine, after the delightful lunch, I thought it was a near-perfect day.

We had only been gone about twenty minutes, merrily strolling along, when the huge elephant came up the bank from the river and blocked our path. At least, some of us were merry. Rose and Mabel were not speaking because Rose had finally gotten up the nerve at lunch to demand that she have separate accommodations from Mabel. Rose told David that she would no longer room with Mabel, either in the tented camp or back at Leopard Dance. Mabel, insulted, also had some choice words for Rose, so the two were not exactly chummy.

The path was well-worn, bordered with tall grass and scrub. Fresh tracks and spoor of numerous animals marked it, including giant balls of elephant dung. The dung beetles were hard at work trying to move those.

"Stand perfectly still and do not speak," whispered

Vincent, his eyes locked on the elephant. "This is his normal path, his territory. We should not have invaded it. If he approaches us, ease backwards, off the path. Move quietly into the weeds." Sliding his rifle from his shoulder, he clicked off the safety.

The elephant's massive ears flapped straight out as he stared at us, a sure sign of irritation. He raised his head and trumpeted. That did it for us, so we each started scooting backwards into the brush, hoping to appease him, or at least remove ourselves from his view. I thought we must be annoying him, as Vincent said, with our intrusive presence.

But I was wrong. We were not the objects of his anger.

Now hidden in the relative safety of the tall grass, I watched the massive beast trumpet again. Then he whirled and charged down the path in the direction of the river toward a small group of armed men, all wearing camouflage clothing. They had emerged suddenly from the reeds of the riverbank. One of the men raised his rifle.

"No!" screamed Mabel, rushing out of the brush and down the path after the elephant, waving her arms. "No. Don't shoot, don't shoot! Hold your fire. Don't shoot him."

The confused beast stopped in his tracks. Then he trumpeted again as he turned back up the path toward Mabel.

Panicked, George snatched Vincent's rifle from his hands, aimed it at the frantic elephant, and fired.

But he didn't shoot the elephant.

He shot Mabel.

25

There was no folkloric performance that night.

Instead, an ambulance came for Mabel's body, and the police came for George.

We were all in shock, particularly those of us who had witnessed the shooting—shocked over poor dead Mabel, over poor little frightened George, over the glimpse of the armed poachers and the sounds of the crazed elephant over all of it. Though Jay, Connie, and Chase had remained behind, they shared our horror and sadness.

The camp was in total chaos. Officials came and went. Everyone was questioned, and dinner was served on trays sent to our tents. We were all ordered to remain inside until the investigation into the shooting was completed. Finally, David sent word for us to be prepared to leave for Leopard Dance at first light.

Poor Mabel's tent had been stripped. Rebecca said her things would be sent with us back to the safari camp, then held until her next of kin could be contacted.

"I know what you're thinking, Sidney," Jay said when we retired to our tent. "I recognize that look on your face."

"What look?" I was staring at my dinner entree of wild game and rice. It would no doubt be excellent, as all the meals had been, but I had lost my appetite. I couldn't eat. I put the lid back on my plate and poured a glass of cool water from the carafe instead.

Jay's appetite was always good, in any circumstances. He had no problem eating.

"The Nancy Drew look," he said as he chewed. "I can see it in your eyes. You want to find out what Mabel knew, don't you? Leave it alone, babe. Don't pick up the baton. Whatever's going on here and at Leopard Dance wasn't Mabel's business and it's not yours, either. We're only in this country for a few days. You don't have to save the world."

I looked him straight in the eye. "I'm not trying to save the world, Jay. But yes, I would like to know what's going on, and what Mabel knew. And yes, I do feel a certain responsibility to carry on her unfinished business. And that's okay. I can't help it. It's who I am."

Jay put his empty plate aside, picked up a corkscrew, and began opening a bottle of wine from the tray. "You can't undo what's happened, Sidney, or turn her tragic death into murder. It was an accident. You saw it. This safari operation may not be on the level, and it may be a cover for something else, but it's not our problem, and irregular or even illegal activity by this outfit is not the same as murder. Remember that what happened today was just a horrible accident, with witnesses. Here, try some of this. Maybe it will help."

He poured me a glass of the wine. I took a sip and leaned back in my chair. "Two people have died, Jay."

His eyes were fixed on me. "Yeah," he said quietly, pouring his own glass, "but one was munched by a hungry cat. The other died because everyone panicked, and because George is a bad shot. I agree that something is not right in this operation, but that's another matter entirely. It's not connected to the two deaths."

"Oh, yes, it is."

"How?"

"I don't know how. I haven't worked that out yet. One death I can buy … maybe. But two just can't be a coincidence. And besides, I have a bad feeling. I can't explain it."

"Look, Madame Zsa Zsa, put away the crystal ball for tonight. I say we're not talking anymore about this until morning. You're upset, I'm upset, and we are both exhausted. Tomorrow, Sidney, we'll talk tomorrow. Now go to sleep, babe, just let it all go."

Draining his glass, he grabbed his tiger-striped pajamas, went into the bathroom and closed the door. I heard the water start, but for once, there was no singing in the shower.

For a few moments, I remained where I was in the chair, sipping the last of my wine, thinking, planning. Then leaving my clothes on, I climbed into bed, turned off my lamp, rolled over facing the wall, and pulled the covers up to my ears.

If Mabel had truly discovered any concrete evidence of funny business surrounding the Leopard Dance operation at this tented camp, I decided, that knowledge had died with her. So if I wanted to know what she had found, I would have to retrace her steps and do a little quiet nocturnal investigating just as soon as the camp slept. It was my only chance. We were leaving in the morning. Morning would be too late.

I heard the bathroom door open, then close. Soon after, Jay's lamp went off. His bed creaked under his weight as Jay stretched out. I thought about Mabel and what she had said to me in the afternoon before the walk that ended her life. I thought of her body, lying on the path, surrounded by the beauty of the African bush.

Tears ran down my face.

"Don't sob, Sidney," Jay said in the darkness. "I can hear you sobbing. Get some sleep, Angel. There's nothing you can do for Mabel now. I have some aspirin in my shaving kit if you want one."

I didn't answer. If I took more aspirin than I had already taken, I'd have to call 911. And there was no 911.

When Jay's deep snoring began, I crawled out of bed and slipped my shoes back on. Then I slid the zipper down carefully, grabbed a flashlight from its holder, and stepping into the darkness, quietly closed the tent behind me.

The moonlight was bright on the path outside the tent. I took a deep breath and decided I would be much safer with the flashlight off. It would have been smart to include Jay in my reconnaissance, but I knew he would never go for it. Not only that, he would try to stop me.

"Curiosity killed the cat" my mother often says to me. Maybe, but slipping along the edge of the path in the moonlight, alert to every sound, this little kitty planned to be ever so careful.

Mabel's death certainly appeared to be an accident. *Still, someone must surely be breathing a little easier*, I thought, *now that Mabel was out of the way*. I intended to discover what Mabel meant when she told me that "something in this camp is rotten." If Mabel could find out, so could I. I felt I owed her that much.

⊬

Picking my way along the path, I walked as quickly as I dared, sticking to the shadows as much as possible. There was no one else out. Everyone seemed to have turned in for the night as instructed

I knew there would be guards somewhere, but guessed that they made regular rounds. Every now and then, as I slipped from shadow to shadow, I stopped to listen. Nothing. No sounds of men, or of beasts beyond the faint rustlings of birds. Only the wind and the buzzing of insects. I was afraid of wild animals, of course, but even more afraid of people. I concocted a story to explain my midnight stroll if I got caught.

I wore the thin, dark gray shirt and black jeans that Jay said made me look like a burglar. It was the perfect outfit for my mission, but not exactly warm. The temperature had plunged with the setting of the sun and the night was cold.

My goal was to check out the office in the main tent. I

had noticed in the afternoon, while enjoying my leisurely lunch with Fernando, that Mabel had taken a super long time returning each time she visited the ladies' room off the dining area. At first I wondered if she was ill, but she seemed completely fine, looking no more out of sorts than usual. So then I wondered why it took her so long to return from the bathroom. Visiting the ladies room myself, I spotted a door marked "office" in a partitioned wall right next to it. My bet was that Mabel had spent all that extra time in the office, not in the restroom. So what had brought Mabel to the office again and again?

The office. That was where I intended to search while the camp slept.

Silently scooting through the night, I cautiously passed the other tents and turned a corner, headed for the main tent. The camp was so hushed that I could hear the faint sounds my own feet made on the sandy path.

It was all silent. Too silent.

Something was wrong.

There should have been some sort of night sounds. There were none. Insects, birds, animals were all around me, but they were still.

Wild creatures fall silent at the approach of man.

Someone was coming.

I saw a faint beam of light on the path behind me.

I sprinted up the final steps to the main tent and ducked behind a post just ahead of the guard. He moved like a phantom on the path below me, but there was nothing ethereal about him. He was a dark, husky man, not quite as big as Vincent, and he was thoroughly and efficiently inspecting the underbrush lining the path with the beam of his light as he made his rounds. His uniform looked almost paramilitary. The moon shone on the barrel of his rifle.

Lucky. That's what *I was.* I was just seconds ahead of him. He had almost caught me. I stood motionless behind the post long after I thought he had moved on. Then I stole through the dark dining area toward the office.

There was no lock on the office door. I entered and closed it softly behind me before I switched on my flashlight. After a quick search through a small desk and a file cabinet, I thought I knew why the office was not locked. There was nothing worth locking up. All I could find was a bunch of invoices for groceries.

So what had brought Mabel to this room again and again?

I began to worry that whatever she had found here had been removed after her death.

Frustrated, I sat in the desk chair and tried to think it out. I started going through the files again, this time more methodically. I was looking for a tip-off, a pattern, something false. Whatever clue was hidden in the files might not be obvious, I thought, but there must be something.

I had almost given up when I suddenly realized what Mabel had found. It had been there all along, hidden cleverly in plain sight, in black and white, before me all the time. Eagerly scanning paper after paper in the beam of my flash, I was so intent on reading that I didn't hear what must have been footsteps approaching in the hallway. The sound of a toilet flushing in the adjacent men's room nearly gave me heart failure.

Switching off my light, I stuffed some of the invoices under my shirt, closed the drawer, and had only just slid behind the door as it opened.

A strong beam of light from the guard's big flash swung around the room, highlighting the filing cabinet where I had been standing seconds earlier.

The guard did not step into the room, so he never saw me behind the door. If he had, I would have been toast. Lucky again.

Apparently satisfied, he switched off his light, pulled the

door closed, and continued his rounds. I heard his footsteps receding toward the dining room.

As soon as I thought he was really gone, I followed suit. As my mother would say, I was out of there before you could say Jack Robinson.

Back through the darkened hall, past the dining room, down the steps, I raced down the path toward my tent. I paused only when I thought I heard an unusual sound, and as I ran I kept a sharp watch for the beam of a flashlight.

I had almost made it to the tent and was looking back over my shoulder when I collided with someone.

For the second time that night, my heart almost failed me as strong hands gripped my shoulders.

"Sidney," George demanded, "what do you think you are doing? Why in the hell are you running around all alone in the dark? This is no time or place for jogging. Are you insane?"

26

"George!" I said as he released my shoulders, blinking at me in the dim light through his big glasses. He looked more owlish than ever. "How did you get here? Where did you come from? I thought you had gone to the station with the police."

"Willem came for me. He brought a lawyer. They arranged my release until the inquest. I will have to return then, but since I am staying on in Africa for a while after the tour anyway; that's not a problem. They all say I'll be fine because everyone knows it was a horrible accident. They just drove me back, after the police took my statement about ... about Mabel." His face looked so sorrowful. "I'll never get over causing her death," he said, with a catch in his voice, "I didn't mean to—"

"We all know that, George," I said, cutting him off, not wanting to hear his sad apology. I felt so bad for him. I knew he must be in agony over what he had done.

"No one is blaming you, George," I went on. "No one. We all understand that it was a terrible accident. You never meant to harm her. You were trying to save her."

"That's kind of you, Sidney. I appreciate you for saying that. I hope everyone sees it that way. I hope they can forgive me."

I had no answer for that. I had forgiven him, but I knew that my view was not shared by all the others. We started walking again on the path and soon reached the turnoff to my tent.

At the entrance of my tent I said softly, "Are you free to go now, George?"

"Yes. Totally. I have been released. The lawyer says that the inquest will only be a formality. I'll be leaving with the group for Leopard Dance in the morning."

"You must be exhausted."

"I am."

I patted his shoulder as I left him to slip back inside and whispered, "I'll see you in the morning, George. Try to get some rest."

Jay was still snoring like a buzz saw beneath his mosquito netting. I crammed the papers I had stolen into my little bag and changed into my pajamas in the dark. I had what I thought might be Mabel's information, but I was simply too exhausted to think about it anymore until morning. I fell asleep the minute I stretched out on my bed.

⅃

The Rovers turned into the now-familiar road to Leopard Dance just before noon.

When we rolled in from our disastrous excursion to the tented camp, Henrik van der Brugge was standing at the reception pavilion to personally welcome us back.

He must have left our camp much earlier, perhaps even in the middle of the night. Or maybe he had flown home early in the morning. Who knew? Although I had not heard a plane or seen an airstrip at the tented camp, one certainly may have been on the property. It was extensive and we hadn't seen it all.

Henrik looked fresh, relaxed, and as handsome as ever. Me, not so much, after only a tiny bit of sleep.

I didn't trust Henrik any more than Jay did, though I still found him mighty attractive. Even so, I had already decided that I wouldn't be sharing any more intimate dinners with him. Been there, done that.

Rebecca and Winsome stood by his side, serving drinks and offering cold, damp towels for our hands and faces. Both were welcome after the long, hot ride. The Leopard Dance team was working extra hard to make us forget the horror we had experienced by the river, as well as to put us all in happier moods.

Most of the group was clearly ready to move on, too, so when van der Brugge issued an invitation to a special farewell dinner at his house, it was greeted with enthusiasm.

"That's great!" Chase said, "What time?"

"Around eight o'clock tonight," he replied, "following your last game drive. You will be driven directly to my home for Sundowners and dinner after you return. Right now, Willem has a simple buffet lunch laid out for you in the dining hall, and then your afternoon is free until the bell rings for the game drive. The spa is open, as is the boutique and the swimming pool. Welcome back, my friends. Please enjoy your day."

An informal salad and sandwich buffet had been set up. Pleading a headache, I chose a sandwich and a drink, borrowed a book from the library, and took it all straight back to good old Hut No.1. Jay lingered over lunch with the others.

I locked the door and unpacked the little overnight bag, remembering to watch for my lost earring. No earring. I even turned the bag inside out. I'd noticed one of my simple silver hoops missing in the vehicle on the way back to camp and I'd hoped it had ended up in my bag somehow. I could have lost it anywhere—on that ill-fated game walk or in my bed, since I hadn't taken the time to remove my jewelry before sleeping. It wasn't valuable but I still hated to lose it.

I took the stolen papers, the book, and my lunch out onto the little deck. The riverbed was quiet, with nothing moving as far as I could see. Jay was going straight from lunch to a spa appointment at 2:00. That gave me just enough private time for my first good look at those papers.

Time, before Mabel's death, had seemed to pass so slowly, with the rhythm of one lazy, pleasurable day easily flowing into another. After the tragedy, it seemed to have accelerated, shifting into fast-forward. Then it seemed that all anyone wanted was to just get the ill-fated trip over and done with as quickly as possible so we could all return to Cape Town and go our separate ways. Everyone had been extremely polite and pleasant over breakfast—respectful, but clearly distancing themselves, preparing to move on. No one talked about Mabel or what had happened to her. Certainly, no one wanted to be held up by an investigation. I didn't, either, but I knew I could not ignore what I had found. I felt I owed it to Mabel.

The papers I had pocketed in the office of the tented camp were invoices—ordinary invoices, as you might find in any hotel or restaurant manager's desk, bills written in English for everything from soap and canned goods to fresh produce. What made these particular invoices interesting was the name, address, and logo on the top of each one, plus the money totals on each.

The money amounts were given in U.S. dollars, not South African rand. As Fernando had told me on the banks of the Limpopo, following the collapse of their currency in 2009, Zimbabwe had begun using the U.S. dollar, abandoning their own currency. These invoices, handwritten with the city, Harare, printed at the top along with the date, were each for large amounts of meat and other common provisions, all at high prices. In dollars. A lot of dollars. Thus, the bills appeared to have originated in Zimbabwe.

Even more interesting was the name of the company doing the invoicing, and the clever logo. The printed letterhead read Spieël Provisioners. The company logo said *Spieël*, and directly under that word, and attached to it, was *lëeips*—*spieël* spelled backwards—in a stylized logo much like the one designed for Leopard Dance. I had been told that the principal owner of Spieël was Henrik van der Brugge.

I wasn't sure what the invoices were for, but I didn't think they were really for groceries.

Willem, I remembered from our cooking talk, had told me that no provisions ever came from Zimbabwe, only from South Africa.

The answer might be found in the Afrikaans dictionary I now held, the same book that had so interested Mabel. I turned to the "S" section and looked up the word Afrikaans word *spieël*.

My guess from the look of the logo was correct. In English, it means "mirror."

The bills were a mirror image of what they actually said. If the bill said the goods were coming from Harare, they were actually going to Harare and so on. I believed that I had found the key to the records of a money-laundering and poaching/smuggling operation. And Mabel must have found it out first.

Just as I was fully exploring that explosive idea, I heard Jay entering the hut. I shoved the invoices under a cushion and sat on it. I wasn't ready to share my newly hatched theory with anyone, even Jay or the authorities, until I had thought it all through.

"Hi," Jay said, poking his red head through the opening in the window wall. "I thought I might find you out here. Look at the yummy things I brought you."

He set a tray with coffee and an array of delightful little treats next to me on the little table.

"How dear of you, Jay! Thank you," I said, biting into a perfect little scone. "This sure brightens up the afternoon. It was really nice of you to fix this tray for me with all these lovely things and bring it all the way here from the dining hall. What made you think of it?"

"Oh, I'm always thinking of you, Sidney. You just don't realize it."

"What's this?" I said, pulling a small white envelope out from under the platter of treats.

"Oh, that's nothing, give it to me," Jay said, trying to grab it.

He was too late. I already had the note out of the envelope. It didn't take long to read it, and even less time to smell a rat.

> I'm sorry you are not feeling well.
> Please enjoy this with my compliments.
> —Willem

I looked up at Jay, who was laughing.

"I should have known," I said.

"Well, it was worth a try. I really would have made you a tray myself, Sidney, if I ran a restaurant, but I don't. Now give me some of that banana bread. It looks good. You aren't mad, are you?"

"No, Jay, not at you. Only at myself, for being so trusting."

"I tell you that all the time, hon, but you never listen."

I could never in a million years explain Jay or our relationship to anyone sane. There's no point in even trying.

"I'm not as trusting as you think. I've decided that I'm not sure what anyone on this trip is up to or even who they really are. Except you and me, of course."

He plopped into the chair next to mine on the deck. "No kidding. They all seemed to be on the level when we first met them, but now I don't know. I can promise you this, lady. Whoever the fakes are, they don't have much imagination. Who would fake being a travel agent when they could pass themselves off as someone more exciting, like a movie star or fashion designer?"

"I'm glad you brought that up, Jay. I've been thinking. Can we talk for a minute about our fellow travelers? We knew almost immediately that Dennis was a phony. We'll probably never know his real story. But what about the others? Let's go down the list. Take Wendy and Tilda, for starters. Do you think they are for real?"

"Yep. They are real all right, I know that for a fact. I was subjected to two solid hours of minutia about their agency back on High Street in Piddling on the Green."

"Jay," I said, shaking my head and laughing, "that's not the name of their village."

"Whatever. It's something like that. They're in the clear. They're real."

"I completely agree. Scratch Wendy and Tilda."

We were both silent for a moment.

"Fernando." Jay spoke his name with his best Italian accent. "What about Fernando, Sidney? I love the idea of suspecting that Italian Romeo."

"He's not a Romeo, Jay. He's nice, and I'm pretty sure he's legit. He tells tons of funny insider airline stories. He knows the biz."

Jay rubbed his chin thoughtfully. "True, but stories can be stolen from someone else. Ask him technical questions the next time you get a chance. See if he has any answers."

I rolled my eyes. "You just want him to be the bad guy," I said. "Admit it. I think he's who he says he is, but okay, we'll check him out further. Who's next? What about Connie?"

Jay grinned. "For real? Can you picture Peaches mixed up with crooks in an international criminal ring? Can you really see that? I can't. Not at all. Besides, she knows too much about the travel business. Connie's not a fake."

I shrugged. "Yeah. I agree. If the poaching ring was after big cats, she might sign on with them for the fur, but I don't think she's into rhino horn. Okay. Not Connie. Who's next?"

"Rose," Jay said.

"No way." We both laughed. We had spoken in unison.

I reached for another sip of coffee but the cup was

empty. I opened the carafe and poured more. "What about Chase and Rich and George?" I said. "We already know Chase and Rich are not agents. They don't claim to be. They supposedly sell travel insurance. Can we find out if they are really with an insurance company? There's no way of checking that out without the Internet, is there?"

"No," Jay said.

"Okay," I said. "That will have to wait until we are back in Cape Town. What do you think about George?"

Jay shook his head. "I just don't see anyone as nervous as George being mixed up in a lot of violence with wild animals, do you? Wild men, too. George is a big chicken. And that same chicken thing applies to Chase. Rich, I don't know anything about. But he wouldn't make a move without Chase. They're inseparable. Whatever they do, they do together."

"True." I paused. "Who's left? David?"

Jay threw back his head and roared with laughter. "You've got to be kidding. Don't be rrrrrridiculous!"

"Well, then, that's the lot, Jay. Not really a suspicious group, is it? I can't see any of them involved in illegal schemes here, can you?"

"No," he said. "I'm not sure everyone is exactly who they say they are, but that doesn't make them criminals, does it?"

"No. It doesn't," I said. "So you think they're all pretty much in the clear?"

"I basically trust our people, Sid, but van der Brugge's operation is another story. I don't trust van der Brugge and his team one little bit. I'm not sure that it matters, though. I'm not sure I care beyond recommending to Silverstein to find another vendor. I think that's as far as our duty goes."

I mulled this over. Was that really where our duty ended? Finally I said, "And we really don't have any hard evidence against them yet, do we?"

Jay gave me a sharp glance. "Sidney ..."

"What?"

"I don't like that 'yet' word. You have that look in your eyes again. Please don't go all Clouseau on me. Let's just enjoy the rest of this safari—despite Dennis and Mabel and whatever else is happening—and then get back to Cape Town and call Diana to nix this as a venue. We just met these people. Their problems are not our business. Who cares? Dial it down, okay? Bye now, I'm going to the boutique."

I didn't promise him anything. I couldn't, because I fully intended to do some more snooping and follow up on my theory as soon as I got a chance.

27

After he left, I walked to the dining hall and found a few of the others lingering over dessert. I got a mug of coffee and joined them, hoping to lay some of my suspicions to rest.

"Feeling better?" Fernando asked.

"Yes, thanks. Lots."

"Good."

"This stuff is divine. Better get yourself some, Sidney," Connie said, spooning more whipped cream onto her dessert from a bowl on the table. "Willem really outdid himself today. Put out the big pot and the little."

George frowned. "What the hell does that mean, Connie?" he said. "Nobody knows what that means. Why don't you speak English?"

"Get Sidney to translate," Rich said. "She speaks Southern."

"Pay no attention to them, ladies," Fernando said in our defense. "Ignore their insults. These are not worldly men. They think everyone should speak as they speak."

He rose from the table with an aside to me. "I'm going to change for a swim. Care to join me?"

"Later, maybe," I said with a smile. "After another cup of coffee."

Everyone headed in different directions, most for naps, some to the gift shop and the spa. I was soon alone at the table.

"More coffee?" It was Willem, coming out of the kitchen with a steaming coffeepot.

"Thanks," I said, as he refilled my cup.

He poured himself a cup and then set the coffeepot down on a stand.

"Mind if join you?"

"No, please, have a seat. Your luncheon was delicious. Everyone said so. And thank you for sending me the tray of treats."

"I'm glad you enjoyed it," he said, smiling. "I was going to bring it to your hut myself, but Jay offered to deliver it. He said he was on his way back, that you were tired, hadn't had much sleep. You must be feeling better now."

His mouth was still smiling, but the sly blue eyes weren't. They were watching me.

"Yes, I am," I replied. "Much better, thanks."

Our conversation was interrupted by Sheba's sawing cough. It was startling, as always.

"She wants out. It is time for her walk. I must go to her. But first, let me say that I am glad you came by, Sidney. I want to return this to you."

He reached into his pocket, brought out a small silver hoop earring, and placed it on the table in front of me.

"My earring. Thank you! I've been looking for it. Where did you find it?"

"One of the busboys turned it in to me. He found it when he was mopping the floor at the tented camp."

"That's great. I'm so glad to have it back. Please thank him for me."

He gave me a searching look, his blue eyes steely. "He found it on the floor of the office. Why would it have been there, Sidney?"

"I have n-no idea," I stammered, thinking fast. "Maybe I dropped it in the dining room and it caught in strands of the mop."

"Perhaps," he said, watching me closely with those hard blue eyes, "or maybe he found it in the office because you dropped it there."

"What reason would I have to be in the office?"

"None. At least, no credible one." He rose to go, still watching me. "I will hate to see you leave tomorrow, Sidney, but perhaps it is for the best. It is difficult for an outsider to understand our ways here in the bush. Things are not always as they seem. You belong to another country, another world, one far safer than this one. It is time for you to return. I hope you've enjoyed your visit, but it's time for your visit to end."

I wasn't sure how to answer, so I warbled out some cheesy goodbye and got out of there before he could ask me any more questions. As I left, I glanced back over my shoulder and saw him still watching me with that intent look. I smiled and waved. He gave me a mocking salute; then he turned to go back into the kitchen.

I pocketed the telltale earring and got the heck out of there.

ℋ

Winsome was folding towels when I found her in the laundry room.

She was friendly and asked if I needed anything, but her whole demeanor changed when I told her that what I really wanted was answers. Her friendly smile vanished, replaced with a worried look.

"Oh, Miss, please, relax and enjoy this beautiful day. Do not ask me questions that I cannot answer. There is nothing here for you to know beyond what you have already seen. Stop worrying, Miss, and it will all be fine. Please believe me, it is all fine."

But it was not all fine. I knew it, and she knew it.

ℋ

Vincent was in the parking area behind the kitchen washing one of the Rovers when I found him.

"No, Miss," he said, with a troubled look in his eyes, "I have not seen Mr. Hsu either here or at the tented camp in many months. When he comes, it is not announced. He just comes. He never stays long, never more than one night. No, I don't know what he does when he comes. It is not my business. I am here to drive the jeeps and help track the animals. I don't ask questions, I just take orders. I go where they tell me to go, do what they tell me to do. I do my job, what I am paid to do, and that's all."

⋇

Rose had no answers for me either, when I visited her hut on the way back to mine, but she did give me something important.

Before we had moved from Leopard Dance to the tented camp, she and Mabel had been roommates. I thought she might have information. She didn't, but she had something else. A clue.

"I'm sorry, Sidney. I'm afraid I'm not much help. She didn't confide in me at all. I didn't like her. She didn't like me. We barely spoke."

"I know that, Rose, but I thought she might have mentioned suspicions she may have had."

"No, and all her things had been removed from the hut when I got back. But I did find this." She handed me a folded piece of paper. "It was mixed in with my things. I've been wondering what I should do about it. You don't think she put it in my bag on purpose, do you? It's hard to believe that she would leave me a message. Like I said, we barely spoke."

I unfolded the paper. It was a printed page torn from the Afrikaans dictionary, the page containing the Afrikaans meanings of English words beginning with the letter "M." The English word "mirror" and the Afrikaans word "spieël" were circled. There was nothing written on it, but folded in with it was a handwritten note.

"She must have, Rose. I think it is a message to you or someone else. It was meant as insurance in case something happened to her."

"And it did."

"Yes," I said, with a shock of remembrance, "it did."

"What do you think it means, Sidney, and what should I do about it?"

"I don't know yet. Time is short," I said, refolding the paper and stuffing it in my pocket. "If you don't mind, Rose, I'll keep this for now. Let me check it out, and I'll let you know what I discover. In the meantime, don't mention this to anyone. It could be dangerous for us both."

28

After leaving Rose's hut, I bumped into Fernando and George on their way to the swimming pool. I was glad my latest clue was safely tucked away in my pocket, concealed from prying eyes.

"Hello, Sidney. Thought you were joining us," George said. "Go get your suit."

Fernando's sharp, dark eyes stared at me.

"She looks as if she has something else on her mind, George," he said. "What's wrong, *cara mia*?"

"Nothing's wrong. I was just having a little girl talk with Rose, that's all."

"Really?" Fernando said. "I didn't realize you were close."

He knew I was lying. Fernando didn't miss much.

"Enough of this chitchat," George whined. "Come on, Fernando. It's too hot to talk here in the sun, and I want a drink. See you at the pool, Sidney."

Fernando gave me another sharp look as he followed George down the path. I waved and headed in the opposite direction.

It didn't take me long to reach the privacy of my hut. I unlocked the door. Jay, I knew, was still at the spa. He had said he would meet us later at the pool for a swim before the game drive.

I turned on the ceiling fan, opened the sliding glass wall on the river side, and closed and locked the sliding shutters. Then I retrieved the invoices from my hiding place. I climbed onto the bed with them and, resting against the pillows, unfolded Mabel's little papers from my pocket. I finally had two solid clues. I had to figure out what they meant before I could decide on my next move.

I thought I recognized the handwriting on the note Rose had found stuffed in her drawer as soon as I saw it. It looked a lot like the writing on the dinner invitation I had received from Henrik. Had Henrik written it? I wished then that I had saved the invitation for comparison.

It had Mabel's name on it. The note read,

> Would you please meet me after dinner this evening to discuss your concerns about the rhino? Winsome will be happy to guide you to me whenever you choose.

It was signed *Ingwe*.

Ӿ

I was still mulling and stewing over what it all meant when Jay returned from the spa.

"Hi, pumpkin. Still not changed? I thought we were going swimming."

"You go on without me, Jay. I haven't even started packing, much less filling out my fam report for Diana."

"It may not be necessary, Sid, if we deep six this place."

I took out my notepad. "She'll want a written report, Jay. She always does."

He shrugged. "Yeah. I guess she does. I got a chance to call New York, by the way, on my way to the spa. I spotted a phone in the office in the dining lodge. The door had been left open. There was no one around, so I just walked right in and used it. I told you there must be one."

"What did she say?" I asked. "Have they signed the contract?"

"She hadn't gotten to the office yet. The time difference, remember? I just left a message for her not to let Silverstein sign it until he could talk with us, unless, of course, he's already signed it. I hope it's not too late."

I sighed. "Sign it without hearing our report first? Then what would be the point in sending us here?"

He shook his head. "You are thinking logically, Sidney, always a mistake when dealing with Diana and Silverstein. He's pretty much sold on this place, love, because the price is right. It's a really good deal for him and you know how cheap he is. I think he just meant for us to figure out how to make it work well for the High Steppers and his other tour groups. The housekeeping and touring details, not the money details. As long as he thinks the basics are acceptable I don't think he cares much about anything else."

I sat down at the desk. "I guess. But remember what he said about holding us personally responsible if anything goes wrong?"

"I remember, and I would have said more on the message for CYA, but Rebecca caught me. She came in and told me that the phone was not for the use of the guests so I had to cut it short."

I tapped my pen on the notepad. "Are you worried about Diana and Silverstein, Jay?"

He shook his head. "No, but when we get back to Cape Town, I'm calling them again just to be sure we are all on the same page. Whatever they decide after that is up to them, not us. We'll have done our job."

I put the pen down, grabbed a brush and began to pull my hair up into a twist. "Good idea. Have fun swimming. I'll be finished in the shower when you get back. I may go for a drink, too, if I'm dressed in time."

"Okay, sweetie, see you later." He opened the door, but then turned to me once more. Looking back at me, he said, "I'm glad you've decided to sit this one out. For once, you're showing some sense in not poking around in stuff. One thing to remember is that whatever happens here in private behind the scenes does not affect the game drives or the accommodations at all. That's all Silverstein cares about. The food and facilities here are really good for the money. As far as the average tourist goes, minding his own business, unlike you, babe, this place is great. If we are too late, if Silverstein has already signed the contract, I say we just blow off our worries about this lodge. The extracurriculars might not matter at all. We don't have any concrete proof, only suspicions, and there's no point in getting everyone all worked up if Itchy is already committed. We'll find out what the status of that is before we tell them all the bad news, okay?"

⚜

I should have showed all my clues to Jay right then and bounced my ideas off of him, but I didn't. We are colleagues and best friends and I love him, but Jay tends to ignore bad stuff in the hope that it will just somehow go away on its own. I knew he had decided to completely ignore all of the terrible things that were happening around us. If I told him what I was doing, what I was thinking, he would not only refuse to help but also try to stop me from investigating.

I decided to enlist George's help before telling Jay about my plans. George might be happy to have a way to lift some of the burden of guilt over Mabel's death from his shoulders. From what he had said to me, I knew his careless action and its terrible consequence weighed heavily on him. In helping to break up a poaching and smuggling operation, he might somehow feel exonerated.

I hadn't found the original dinner invitation from Henrik that Winsome had delivered to my room but thought that the handwriting was a pretty close match to the note

Rose found hidden in her things. I felt that, by leaving the note with the page torn from the dictionary, Mabel meant to prove who was behind it all: Mr. Henrik van der Brugge, principal owner of Leopard Dance, the Pearl Moon tented camp, and Spieël Provisioners.

I found George at the bar, on his second or third drink. George seemed to be spending more and more time in the bar, bending Willem's ear, particularly since the accident. I would have bet that Willem was tired of talking to him and would be glad to see him return home as well.

George made a visible effort to focus on me through his big red glasses. "Hi, George. Looks like you're all alone. May I join you?"

"Sure, have a seat. When Willem returns, he'll get you a little drink. Might be fifteen minutes or so. He said he had to go feed Sheba, whoever that is."

I sat next to him. "It's okay. I don't need a drink. I came to talk to you. I have something I want to show you."

I pulled out my papers to show him. "George, listen to me, it's important. I need your full attention. George, you aren't drunk are you?"

He shrugged and smiled a little lopsided smile. "Not really. No more than usual. What's on your mind?"

I hesitated for a moment, but then decided that he was sober enough to hear what I had to say, and to help me if he chose to do so. I thought he might, and I knew for sure that Jay wouldn't.

So I spilled my guts to George about the whole deal, relating all my suspicions about Henrik van der Brugge—how I thought Leopard Dance and the tented camp were really a front for a poaching operation.

"I came to you with this," I said, "because I know you meant Mabel no harm, and that you've been distraught over her death. I thought that if you could help me expose all of this, it might, in some small way, help you feel better about the accident."

George's eyes teared up, and he took off the red glasses and wiped them with a bar napkin.

"You're right, Sidney, it would," Willem said, approaching us from the room behind the bar. "You should help her, George. We'll both help her. Forgive me for eavesdropping, Sidney. I heard what you said, and if what you say is true, I want to help, too. I can't say I'm shocked. I've had my own suspicions for some time. Could I see those papers?"

I handed them over.

Willem studied them, frowning.

"There are whole files of them, Willem," I said, "in the office at the tented camp and probably in the office here, too. They appear to be ordinary invoices, mixed in with the real ones, but it's perfectly clear what is going on, once you understand the code. Mabel figured it out first, but she didn't tell anyone. This is just a sample. There are lots more. Those files are the records of all the illegal transactions. The paper trail."

All the time I was speaking, George hadn't said a word. He just sat on the barstool blinking, his head swiveling between me and Willem. Watching Willem. Watching me. He looked more like an owl than ever.

A tear rolled down his cheek. He took off the big glasses and wiped his eyes.

"Well. This is quite incriminating, isn't it?" Willem said. "It's not all the proof that will be needed but it is certainly enough to start the investigators on the right path. We must get all this into the proper hands immediately. I will do all I can to make that happen. You will, too, won't you, George?"

"Yes, 'course I will," George slurred, after a pause. He was drinking again, having reached behind the bar and poured himself a double. "I'll help. I guess I must."

Willem took the bottle from him, shaking his head, and replaced the cap.

"George," he said, "before you can be of help to anyone, you need to go to your hut, lie down for a while, and get yourself together." He gave me a conspiratorial look. "Maybe Sidney will walk with you. I am working just now in the kitchen, preparing for tonight."

George just sat there, his head in his hands.

"Sidney," Willem said, suddenly, "I've just had an idea. I've thought of something that you might want to see, something that may help us in exposing this whole operation. I can't take you there now because I am busy with the refreshments for the party tonight, but I can later, during the evening game drive. Why don't you and George meet me back here when the bell rings and I'll take you there myself? Is that okay with you. George?"

George nodded yes, then we stood and walked to the door. He didn't seem so very drunk now, just sad.

"Keep those papers safe, Sidney," Willem added, "and don't tell the others of your suspicions. You never know here who might be listening or who you can trust. Just say you don't feel up to the game drive, that you'll join them at the party later. We'll be finished with everything well before Henrik's party, and before the night is over, I expect that we'll have quite a surprise for him."

29

I had a hard time convincing Jay to go on the evening game drive without me, particularly because he was terrified of the Sundowners. He'd sworn he was never going to another al fresco cocktail party in Africa.

I finally got him to leave with the others by reminding him that David had said that the drinks for this special farewell Sundowner would be served "in a *gaily strrrrrriped* tent on Mr. van der Brugge's lawn" before dinner, not in the bush. Therefore, there would be little chance for a wild animal to attack him. During the game drive itself, he could stay safely in the Rover. I felt bad about deceiving him, but it had to be done.

"George is too drunk to go," I said. "He's lying down. My headache's better, but not completely gone. I'll check on George after a while and we'll meet you later at the dinner party."

"Okay, Sidney. Sorry your head hurts. Take it easy, babe. Don't worry about George. He can take care of himself. You try to grab little nap, too, while we're gone. See you later."

When the bell stopped ringing and I thought everyone had left, I headed for George's hut and knocked on the door. It wasn't long before he poked out his spiky little head. He looked terrible and I could tell that his head must be hurting, but he seemed sober enough.

Together, we walked to the dining hall to meet Willem.

The sun was just setting as we drove out the back gate, loaded in Willem's jeep. George was sprawled in the backseat, complaining about his headache, and I rode shotgun. It promised to be a beautiful evening.

"Where are we headed, Willem?" I shouted over the sound of the engine and the rushing air in the open vehicle.

"You'll see soon enough," he shouted back, steering the jeep around a hole in the dirt road. "Too loud to explain now. Enjoy the ride."

I did enjoy the ride. It was our last evening on safari, and I had hated to give up the game drive. I only agreed to it because I thought what I was doing was more important.

As we lurched off the main road onto a grassy track, I suddenly realized that I hadn't missed my game drive after all. Animals are everywhere in a game reserve. Cruising through the bush in the open jeep, I was getting my own game drive. Willem slowed, reaching across me to point out giraffe moving gracefully in the distance, silhouetted against the setting sun.

The sun had slipped well below the horizon, and the sky was beginning to darken, so Willem turned on the headlights. In a few moments, just as it began to get really dark, he pulled into a clearing and switched off the lights and the engine.

"We're here. Let me help you down, Sidney. George, are you ready? Get it together, George. You'll have to manage for yourself. I've got Sidney. Come on, George, get out of the car." Willem lifted me down. Then, just as my feet touched the ground, George jumped down behind me, suddenly quite sober, and stuck a gun in my back.

30

"This won't work, Willem," I said, as he forced me farther into the clearing. He had taken the gun from George and now had it firmly wedged in my side. "I'll be missed. Before long, they'll all come looking for me."

I could hardly see where I was going in the dim light of the moon. I was terrified.

"It will work, Sidney. It's already working, darling. They won't miss you until morning. You told them yourself that you weren't going on the game drive, didn't feel well. Winsome will back up that story. Winsome is my girl, not Henrik's, though he doesn't know it. Winsome will tell everyone that you are ill, resting in the infirmary. She'll say that you called her to say that you felt worse after they left, and didn't feel up to attending the farewell party at The Big House. She'll say you have a high fever, are delirious, confused. Then, when they hear you have wandered off into the bush alone, no one will be surprised."

He shoved me to the ground with the gun pointed directly at me. "Lie still, Sidney, or I will have to really hurt you. Turn over on your back. Be still, I say, or I'll hurt you so much that you'll be glad when I shoot you. Get busy, George, there's not much time before I have to be back."

George began tying my hands and feet to short stakes that had been previously driven into the ground. He knew exactly what he was doing. It was not the first time.

Stretched between the stakes, I soon could not move at all, except my head.

"You really can't get away with this, Willem," I said, a tremor in my voice. "Someone will come."

"Oh, but I can. Scream if you like. No one will hear you. By the time you are missed, by the time they do come, it will be too late. We are in the leopard's territory and there is a pride of lions nearby. It won't take long. It's dark, and the animals are hungry. As soon as we're finished here, George and I will go to the party and confirm Winsome's story. Later, when the animals have done their work, we will return to remove the ropes and stakes and report the discovery of yet another unfortunate accident."

Willem stood over me, peering down into my face. Even in the shadow I could see his blue eyes glittering. "I'm sorry you had to meddle in all this, Sidney," he said. "I hate to have to do this to you, but you've left me no choice. I can't risk losing what I've built. I was actually quite attracted to you. You are a beautiful woman. In another time, another place … I really liked you, Sidney. George did, too, didn't you, George? We both liked you until you got in our way."

George wouldn't look at me, hadn't looked at me even as he forced me to the ground and tied the knots. Willem kept his gun trained on my head.

"Willem, for God's sake," I pleaded, "don't leave me like this. Or at least, just go on and shoot me before … before … Have some mercy, please. George? *Please*. Can't you stop this? Can't you help me? Please help me."

But George turned away, heading for the jeep. He never looked back, wouldn't meet my eyes.

"Before what? Before the animals come?" Willem laughed. "And deprive you of the suspense? Of your last few moments in this world? No, Sidney, I'm afraid not. You see, I can't afford to leave any evidence. I can't chance that a bullet might be traced back to me. This way, there's no clue as to what really happened. Just as with Dennis, they'll conclude that nature was the culprit."

Terrified as I was, I knew I had to try to keep him talking, to buy some time, in the desperate hope of changing his mind, or that someone might come along in time to save me.

"Did Henrik order you to do this to me?"

"Henrik?" he laughed. "Do you really think Henrik could plan all this? He has nothing to do with my operations. Henrik doesn't give me any orders, except what to cook. Henrik has no idea what's happening under his very eyes."

He smiled as if to himself, his eyes gleaming.

"But he'll know soon enough," he continued, "when I have everything in place. That's when he'll meet with his own accident. Maybe in that plane of his. You see, Henrik doesn't care, has never cared, about the little people, Sidney. He cares only for himself, only for his own desires. Henrik never gave the slightest thought as to what it might mean when he took my wife from me.

"Your wife—"

"Became his wife. You've met her, remember? When she wrecked her car and broke up your dinner party? But it didn't last. Now she's found another husband, a richer one, and only comes around to torment him. Perhaps she imagines she still loves him, especially when she's been drinking. Serves him right. Tell me, Sidney, why did you suspect Henrik?"

"Winsome. She warned me about him. She said I must 'stay away from Ingwe. Ingwe is a bad man.' "

"She did, did she?" he laughed. "Is that what she said? You little fool. *I'm* the one they call Ingwe. *Willem* is Ingwe, not *Henrik.*"

"What about the note?"

"What note?"

"Henrik wrote the note to Mabel, and signed it Ingwe."

"I wrote that."

"But the handwriting … it was the same as in the other note—the one inviting me to dinner."

"I wrote that note, too," he said, "at Henrik's bidding. I had Winsome slip it under your door." His lips stretched into something like a smile. "Ah. That's what made you so certain Henrik was Ingwe."

"Willem, please let me go. I've not done anything to harm you."

"No, dear, and that's the shame of it. But you would, knowing what you know, if I released you. I can't risk that. Not now, when I'm so close to getting everything I want. You shouldn't have meddled in my business. I really have no choice here. You see that, don't you? You're a bright girl. Don't blame me. It's too bad, but it's not my fault. It's your own fault, Sidney. Your own fault. You did this to yourself."

And with another raucous laugh, he climbed into the jeep with George and drove away.

Later, lying still, spread-eagled alone in the moonlight after struggling in vain against the ropes that bound me, those words, "your own fault," echoed in my ears.

His mocking words and my own prayers drowned out the sounds of the night. Eventually my sobs subsided. Numbed by shock and cold, I lay helplessly beneath the stars in the vast African sky. Too late I realized how the whole scheme worked, and what a fool I had been.

31

A snuffling sound heralded the first animal I heard as I lay motionless under the Southern Cross. Then the gray bulk of an elephant emerged from the brush, walking softly as he grazed not twenty feet from me.

Thank You, God, thank you for the elephant.

Lions don't like to come where there are elephants.

I am not afraid of the elephant, Lord, only the lion. The elephant will not harm me if I lie still. *Not unless he steps on me.*

The elephant knew I was there. He has a keen sense of smell. But he paid no attention to me, and after a long while, he moved slowly on. I breathed again, staring at the stars. I could feel ants crawling in my hair.

Then I heard another sound.

A man, this time, I was sure it was a man, walking quietly toward me through the brush. Helpless and desperate as I was, I remained silent until I could figure out who it was.

The brush parted and the moonlight reflected in George's red glasses.

"I can't do it, Sidney," he said. "I can't leave you here like this, no matter what he does to me."

♓

It took a long time and a bit of luck to free me from the ropes and stakes that bound me to the earth. George had done his job too well. The untying was not easy or quick.

Once free, I stretched my aching limbs until, with his help, I could finally stand and hobble forward in the moonlight. Then I walked, and finally ran, following him, for we knew that time was short and our chance of survival slim.

I followed him toward the camp. He knew the way, leading me across a faint trail.

We ran as fast as we were able, fending off branches, dodging obstacles. Broken clouds had formed, partially obscuring the moon.

A deep cough broke the silence. For a moment we paused, slowing to a walk, looking over our shoulders, scanning the bush for movement.

When we saw the eyes glowing in the darkness behind us, I knew deep in my core that this time we would not escape, would not survive, but we ran silently on, ragged gasps and sobs and pounding feet our only sounds, dodging in and out of shadows, on and off the sandy track, stumbling, falling over roots and branches, falling—only to drag ourselves up to run again, to make one final desperate dash for freedom.

But always the eyes were there behind us, coming, coming, ever closer, ever closer, until it was certain that we could not make it, would not elude our fate.

The game was up, the hourglass empty, the tiny bit of luck we once held, gone. Then, though he was far stronger, George inexplicably slowed, falling behind me, shouting to me, "Run, Sidney, run!"

We had almost made it back to the lodge when he was caught. But almost was not enough.

The last sound he made was the terrified squeal of a shoat that tapered off into a deadly silence, a silence broken only by the tearing of flesh and the crunch of bone.

32

The aftermath was terrible, but not as bad as it could have been. Because of Jay. Jay took charge of me and everything else, and it was only later that I fully realized what a masterful job he had done.

I pretty much had a breakdown after my ordeal. I was recovering from shock and distraught over George's supreme sacrifice. Jay thought my sorrow over George's demise was excessive and pointed out that it was George who had put me in danger in the first place. But I couldn't help the way I felt.

George had acted as Willem's main man and his spy, posing as a perennial guest to watch for trouble from people such as Dennis, Mabel, and me. George had purposely killed Dennis on Willem's orders, and Mabel, too, seizing the opportunity of the panicked elephant on the path to make it look like an accident. The two of them had already decided to take her out at first opportunity before she could harm them or their operation. The elephant encounter simply provided an easy way to do it.

"They are pretty sure it was George who killed the man in the Nellie garden as well, Sidney, on orders from Willem. Remember, you saw George that night in the garden just after you saw the mystery men questioning Henrik. The murdered man was said to be a drug runner from Mozambique, but in reality, he was an investigator, like Dennis, working undercover. Both George and Willem were deeply involved in a lot of bad stuff."

I saw Jay's point, but still knew that my life would have

ended had it not been for George. He had come back for me, and I would never forget that.

For the first time in my life, I really could not cope with anything at all for a few days. Jay took care of me. It was Jay who summoned the police and medical people pronto, Jay who got us all back to Cape Town. Jay managed it all. I don't even remember the trip back.

When I finally recovered enough to ask questions and give my statement, we learned that the authorities had been watching the Leopard Dance/Spieël Provisioners operation for quite some time.

"It was my decision, Miss Marsh," the chief investigator said, "to send Dennis Bagwell in undercover, posing as a travel agent, to investigate. I deeply regret losing him. He was a good agent and a fine man. He knew the risks and he had been in the service for many years. Willem killed him when he got too close, leaving him staked out for the leopard as he did you. His autopsy showed marks consistent with that on what remained of his wrists and ankles. They must have had their eye on you for some time, Miss Marsh. I'm not sure how, but you apparently attracted their attention early on as a potential troublemaker. It was also George who stole your key card and searched your hotel room in Cape Town."

"Well, what about Winsome? I understand that she was involved with Willem as well."

"Miss Winsome quickly cut a deal with us to testify against Willem. She was only a minor player in the operation, but she knew all that was going on. The only overt thing she did, as far as we now know, was to steal the memory card from the English sisters' camera. Then she left the hut open so the monkeys would be blamed. Willem ordered her to take the camera card after the sisters had photographed one of his associates. Miss Winsome knew all of this. Her testimony will be most valuable to us when we go to trial."

I was told later that the most important thing they

GAME DRIVE

learned from Winsome was that Willem had ordered George to kill Mabel and make it look like an accident. As we all learned, he succeeded. The elephant made it easy for quick-thinking George. Vincent, whose weapon had been used, was an innocent pawn. He had nothing to do with it. I was glad of that.

The powerful-looking black guy I saw in the garden and later in the ditch—Sylvester, from Zimbabwe—was an associate of Willem's. He is now in jail, along with his boss. Henrik told the police that Willem said Sylvester was a "provisioner," and I guess that really was, technically, correct.

Henrik van der Brugge turned out to be a fairly innocent victim in the whole thing. He is back at the game lodge, trying to rescue his business from the shambles it has become.

"I wouldn't waste a lot of sympathy on him, Sidney," Jay said. "The investigator told me that ol' Henrik made a fortune for himself in diamond mining before he opened the game lodge, so he's got plenty of cash. They're still looking into the details of all that. That's why he wasn't too worried about the game lodge making a profit. He didn't depend on it to support his lifestyle, which is why he gave Willem free rein."

"Did he get a cut of the poaching operation, too, Jay?"

"I don't think so. All the poaching profit was going to Willem, not Henrik. But remember, too, that Henrik was the one who hired Willem, and Willem was there a long time. Henrik's spoiled, but he's not stupid. He might have known something was going on and just turned a blind eye as long as it didn't create problems for him. He seems in the clear, but no one really knows for sure. Only time will tell if he was or not."

After I staggered into Henrik's party and collapsed, weeping and shrieking about George, Willem had made a run for it. They soon caught him and now he was in jail, awaiting trial.

The rest turned out to be exactly who they said they

were—travel agents and airline and insurance reps. They were all sorry, and shocked, and kind.

Leopard Dance was closed until further notice, but we were told that it would reopen in time for the High Stepper's safari. Van der Brugge's lawyer said Silverstein's contract with them for the African tours would hold.

Jay said his piece about that, too. "That's what he gets, Sidney, he and Diana, for booking with the cheapest lodge they could find, and for signing the papers before hearing from us. Serves them right."

"But up until all hell broke loose," I said, "you had a good time at Leopard Dance, didn't you, Jay? I did."

"Yes, but there are lots and lots of other game lodges, Sidney. Much nicer ones. Really great ones. Next time, I'm going to be sure we book one that's more my style."

33

Jay was pacing up and down the hotel room in Cape Town. He always paces in times of crisis. But this time the crisis was mine.

"At least we don't have to check out another game lodge for Diana and Silverstein for the High Steppers tour. I was really worried we'd have to do that. That's good news. Try to focus on that, Sidney."

I was absolutely sick. After all I'd been through, and just when I'd thought it was all over, that I could finally go home to the tiny apartment I love in New York, the police said no.

The police detective had called the hotel two days before my flight home to say that I should not leave the country in case I had to testify. The case against Willem and his operation was more far-reaching than originally thought, and I was right smack in the middle of it. Me and my damn curiosity.

"I think you should call them up and throw a big hissy fit. Don't say you are really, really pissed because that sounds so 'country.' Just be dignified and refined, like the Queen, and say, 'I am not pleased.' It's worth a try."

I groaned and put a pillow over my head in the darkened room. Chocolate. I needed chocolate. Or my mother. No, not my mother. She would say "I told you so."

"The bad news," Jay continued, "is that Diana said Silverstein won't pay your per diem if you stay here to testify. He will hold your job open, and pay the change fee for your return flight, so that's something."

"Not much," I mumbled from under the pillow. I thought about my dear little apartment back in New York. I thought about my rent. I peeked out. "What about my regular pay? Will I get a paycheck?"

"You have to use your vacation days. You get paid for that. Once they're used up, if it goes beyond that, sorry. Too bad, so sad."

Not chocolate or my mother. Alcohol. I needed alcohol.

"That's not all. Diana says that after I leave your hotel room is not in her budget, either. Maybe van der Brugge will put you up at his house. I could ask."

"Jay. I'm not going anywhere near that game lodge."

"Sidney, the guy likes you, and we're pretty sure he's okay after all, remember? At least they haven't found anything to hang on him yet. Plus, it's safe now that Willem and his gang are all in jail. They won't be at the game lodge."

He looked down at me on the bed. "Maybe you could open up a detective agency, Sidney," he said, his eyes dancing, "to pick up a little cash. You just love detecting, don't you, girl? They're all pretty pleased with you for figuring out the scheme Willem was running and giving them the paperwork to prove it."

"Yeah, right. Figured it out, that's what I did. And then what did I do? Went right to George of all people and told him all about it, and thought what a bright little girl I was to figure it all out. Some detective I turned out to be. I always seem to pick the wrong horse. Maybe the Marsh Curse is mutating. Go ahead and laugh, Jay. I know you want to, it's okay. I deserve it."

My future looked dark. In fact, it looked dismal.

The phone rang.

Jay reached for it, saying, "It must be important. I asked them downstairs to screen all the calls."

"Helloooooooo. Star Witness Central, Jay speaking."

There was a pause.

"Who? Oh, heavens, yes! She'll talk to her. Put her on."

He clamped his hand over the receiver. "Sidney, sit up. You'll want to take this."

"Who is it? I told you I didn't want to talk to anyone."

"It's Brooke," he hissed, "your fairy godmother. You have to take her call."

If there is one person I will always talk to in this world it is Brooke. Right at that moment, I needed her wise advice more than ever. I flung the pillow aside and grabbed the phone.

"Brooke! It's so good of you to call! How did you find out about all this mess? The local newspaper? Oh, yeah, I forgot about the newspaper. Yeah, I guess it will probably get picked up by everyone else, too."

Jay said in a stage-whisper, "Maybe you'll have to go into Witness Protection, Sidney. These are bad dudes you are testifying against."

"Just a minute, Brooke." I covered the receiver. "Will you hush? I can't hear. Sorry, Brooke, Jay was talking and I couldn't hear that last thing you said."

I listened for a long while without comment, then thanked her from the bottom of my heart and hung up.

"What did she say? Tell me. Tell me now."

"She said a lot, bless her heart, but the main thing is that she's sending a car for me in an hour. I get to leave. I'm transferring to the Nellie, until I sail with her in her suite on *The Rapture of the Deep* to the Seychelles. From there, after a little R&R on the beach, I can fly back to New York. She really is a fairy godmother."

"What? How can you do that? What about the police? What about the trial?"

"When she found out about everything, Brooke hired a high-powered local lawyer to represent my interest. He made some calls, and now I'm free to go. The trial won't be for months. I can return if I have to testify in person, but they may have enough without me."

I got out of bed and started packing my stuff before heading for the shower.

"What about Diana and Silverstein and Itchy? What are you going to do about them?"

"Brooke called Silverstein and squared everything with him. She pointed out that my new lawyer felt that I was due some recuperation time for the trauma I suffered while on a job for him. Plus, she reminded him of all the great publicity the agency has gotten from my little ordeal."

"Oh. And he was okay with that?"

"Yes."

Then he asked the question that I knew had been foremost in his mind since I told him about Brooke's call. "Well, Sidney, what about me?"

"I'm sorry, Jay, but even fairy godmothers have limits. When Brooke asked about you, Silverstein signed off and turned the call over to Diana. Diana told Brooke that if you intended to keep your job, you would have to return as scheduled so you could escort the High Stepper's Fall Foliage tour to Branson. I'm sorry, honey. I really hate it after all you've done for me. Brooke is sorry, too, but it's out of her hands. She said to tell you."

"That ..."

I don't know all the words Jay used just then to express his feelings about Silverstein and Diana. He used those same words and more, later, when I thanked him again, and kissed him goodbye. I let him vent, but then I had to be going. He accompanied me to the street, where I climbed into the limo and rolled away, bound for The Nellie, and Brooke, and ultimately, for *The Rapture of the Deep* to see if a certain Greek captain was still at her helm.

I've never heard some of the words Jay used and hope I never will again. They were bad words, Yankee curses far, far worse than even a dog-cussin' is Down South.

Let's just say, he was not pleased.

Author's Note

Readers who want to know more about the tragic plight of endangered rhinos and African elephants—or would like to join in effort to save the elephant and the rhino, spearheaded by Britain's Prince William—are encouraged to read news on the subject from the international media. Current articles will also be quoted and posted from time to time on my website, www.mariemooremysteries.com. Also, please visit the following websites for more information or to contribute to the cause:

The National Geographic Society
www.nationalgeographic.com

The International Union of Conservation of Nature
www.IUCN.org

The Tusk Trust
www.tusk.org

World Wildlife Fund (WWF)
www.worldwildlife.org

Photograph by Chad Mellon

Marie Moore is a native Mississippian. She graduated from Ole Miss, married a lawyer in her hometown, taught junior high science, raised a family, and worked for a small weekly newspaper—first as a writer and later as Managing Editor. She wrote hard news, features, and a weekly column, sold ads, did interviews, took photos, and won a couple of MS Press Association awards for her stories.

In 1985, Marie left the newspaper to open a retail travel agency, and for the next fifteen years, she managed the agency, sold travel, escorted group tours, sailed on nineteen cruises, and visited over sixty countries. The Sidney Marsh Murder Mystery Series was inspired by those experiences.

Marie also did location scouting and worked as the local contact for several feature films, including *Heart of Dixie*, *The Gun in Betty Lou's Handbag*, and Robert Altman's *Cookie's Fortune*.

In mid-1999, because of her husband's work, Marie sold her travel agency and moved to Jackson, MS, then New York City, Anna Maria Island, FL, and Arlington, VA. She and her husband now live in Memphis, TN, and Holly Springs, MS.

Game Drive is the sequel to Marie's first novel, *Shore Excursion*, which introduced amateur sleuth Sidney Marsh. For more information, go to:

www.mariemooremysteries.com.

CPSIA information can be obtained at www.ICGtesting.com
Printed in the USA
LVOW11s0008270415

436195LV00001BA/8/P